BLOOD BANK

Maze Leigh

CONTENTS

BLOOD BANK BLURB

For humans to marry, one must be offered to the vampires…

From a young age, I knew where my life would lead. I'd one-day marry and live a happily ever after, but the plan goes awry in a strange twist of fate.

Instead of planning my wedding, I'm preparing to be offered to the vampires. But those unexpected plans add yet another layer of bewilderment.

There are secrets within the walls of the castle—secrets that pull me in many directions and could determine my fate.

I must secure a blood match. If I fail, I will be met by a slow and painful death. If I succeed, I could end up with everything I never knew I wanted.

Dear reader,
Thank you for picking up this book!
I hope you enjoy this adventure where everything is possible,
including magic.
I should warn you this isn't your typical fantasy romance
book.
I will also leave you with this note, I like cliffhangers.
Take that information how you will and read on!
P.S. Make sure to join my newsletter so we can stay
connected!
Much love,
Maze

Prologue

The hum of music filled the air while my hands were fast at work braiding my best friend's hair. Today, we'd celebrate a wedding. Not only a wedding but an offering too. The beat of the music sped up. Soon we'd have to join them. They couldn't start without the bride after all.

"Will you add this to my hair, Veronica?" my best friend Libby said, picking up a string of flowers from her lap and handing it to me.

"Of course, anything for the bride to be," I teased, grabbing the flowers from her hand.

Her cheeks reddened at my jab as I wrapped the flowers around her braid, securing it tight so it wouldn't come loose. With one last look, I brushed the braid over her shoulder, giving her time to examine herself.

"It's beautiful. Thank you!" Her high-pitched voice brought a smile to my face.

Her gown, as white as pure snow, twirled around her as she moved to examine herself in the mirror. Everything about today was going to be marvelous. Libby would marry the love of her life, her stomach already showing slightly from getting too spirited with activities prior to marriage—but the baby would be born into a loving family.

"We should head on down before your soon-to-be husband thinks you bailed." I held out my arm to the girl on cloud nine.

"He would never think that!" she replied, hooking her arm in mine as we left the safety of the bedroom.

We took it slowly, not wanting her to trip from her dress as we descended the stairs to the main floor.

"Wow, look how beautiful you are!" Libby's neighbor spoke, inching forward to cup Libby's face. "Doesn't this make you excited about your own wedding, Veronica?"

I nodded in reply. They expected me to marry. There was already a man picked out who would be my match. The only thing that I would miss after I held my wedding would be my sister.

"We need to head on out before everyone gets worried," I spoke up, tugging Libby out of the grasp of the woman, who was intent on doing a full examination of my best friend.

She was a perfectionist and wanted to make a good impression. After all, we had guests in town.

"Right, we have a tradition to uphold."

Indeed, we did. A tradition that had been in place for hundreds of years. Traditions that we had no plan to break today. I led Libby outside to the waiting arms of those who'd do the final touches to make sure she was beyond beautiful before she walked down the aisle. With a quick kiss of good luck, I scurried over to my seat. I didn't want to miss her grand entrance.

"How does she look?" a voice whispered at my side as I sat down at the front.

"Marvelous—do you expect anything less?" I shot back, sticking out my elbow to jab my little sister in the side.

"Just think, this will all be happening for you soon." Her teasing caused me to whirl on her.

A smile spread across my face as I took in Rory, my little sister, her hazel eyes filled with mischief, her own light brown hair in an updo for the special occasion.

"Be quiet, the both of you," our father hissed out, sat on the other side of me.

I reached out and grabbed Rory's hands. She leaned into my side as we both turned to watch Libby walk down the aisle. The music slowed and we waited for the grand entrance of the soon-to-be married woman. My mouth dropped as Libby appeared, the crowd growing quiet.

Even though I'd just seen her, even helped her get ready, it was different seeing her surrounded by the decorations hung up for the wedding. I watched my best friend make her way down the aisle to stand beside Sam the man who wanted nothing else but to marry her. My smile grew. Tears threatened to spill as their commitment to each other chimed in the air. The wedding was only one part of the celebration. What followed was another joyous event.

In order for one person to marry, one must be offered in exchange. It was the treaty we'd signed with the vampires long ago. The offering would go off to live a new life, one of luxury, and not have to worry about mundane things in life. I squeezed Rory's hands. As Libby's sister was her own offering, Rory would be mine when it came to my marriage. We had traditions to uphold, after all.

CHAPTER 1

"Aren't you excited, Veronica, for your wedding?" my mother prodded as she helped me get fitted in my wedding dress—a dress of a light blue color with jewels sewn all about, a dress fit for the mayor's daughter. But even though the dress was marvelous and it would honor me to wear it, I was indifferent to my wedding.

Only a month ago Libby's wedding had highlighted the love and commitment Libby and her man had for each other so all could see. But for me it was different. I would marry Jax because it was arranged, and that was it. Our fathers deemed it the best match to help keep the balance in the towns. I couldn't just up and marry whoever I pleased. No, each wedding was planned because each marriage came at a cost.

"You don't know Jax that well, but you guys will grow to love each other. Like how your daddy and I did."

Mother might be right; only time would tell. He seemed like someone who wouldn't annoy me, but he also didn't seem like the guy who would drive me crazy with passion either.

Twirling my long brown hair around, I threw it over my shoulder to inspect myself in the mirror, moving side to side to study myself. The dress had an open back, and allowed my figure to be shown off quite nicely, as it hugged my waist but it flowed straight down afterward into a small train at the back, and overall it was comfortable to walk in.

"Rory, what do you think?" I asked as I looked over at my sister, who sat by the window.

She had started to mentally drift away the closer we got to my wedding. We used to be so close, but the past few months it was just different. We still spoke often, but I could tell her heart wasn't there. Her mind was lost in her thoughts, but she refused to share them with me.

"It's beautiful," she mumbled, only giving me a quick glance before leaving the room.

I frowned as she closed the door behind her. What was going on? I'd chosen a blue dress because it was her favorite color. I wanted to honor her and her sacrifice at my wedding. Because without it, there would be no wedding.

Growing up, this had always been the plan and dream we formed together. While Rory loved the town and the people, she'd always wanted more from life. She wanted to explore and see what the world had to offer, and not be content to just settle down and marry someone who was picked for her. Volunteering to be my sacrifice for my wedding would allow her that. As a sacrifice, she'd be offered up to the vampire clan that kept the neighboring towns of humans in check. Without their protection, we'd be cast into battles not only between humans and vampires but between humans and humans as well. It was better to surrender a bit of our control for overall good and peace. And while it was a sacrifice for the town because we'd lose a female, it was an honor for the girl. It was rumored they became lovers of vampires, getting to experience a whole new view of the world. Vampires spoiled their lovers with wealth and fulfilled their every desire. Because of their unique tastes and long life, they took lovers often.

But something must have changed, causing her to second-guess her decision from all those years ago. It would be too late to find another female to be my sacrifice, because all were spoken for. And while we could force another family to take Rory's place, Father wouldn't allow it. He kept his word no matter what.

"Mother, I think I'm going to spend some time with Libby."

My best friend would be the best person to seek input from because her sister was also offered when she got married. She would understand and maybe provide some solutions so Rory and I could spend our last few days together like how it was when we were younger.

I grabbed at the dress straps that lay on my shoulders and yanked them down, allowing the dress to fall as I wiggled my way out. It was not a dress that was hard to put on, which was my type of clothing. While I liked to get dressed up from time to time, the practicality of a garment would always win over its beauty.

With the dress picked up from the floor, I laid it out on my bed before grabbing the garments next to it—a simple pair of black pants and a white shirt.

"You should wear dresses more often, especially for a lady of your stature."

I rolled my eyes. With a quick kiss on her cheek, I turned to leave the room. It would do no good to have this argument with her, as it was a daily battle between us. I just was not as girly as she would have liked. If she ever found out that I could fight and handle a blade, I was sure it would cause her to faint. It would also grant me quite a few smacks and a stern yelling, hoping to set me on the "correct" and "proper" path of being a lady.

A soft sigh escaped my lips. Life was simpler a month ago when Libby was the main focus. Now, everyone had their eyes drawn to me and making my wedding perfect.

The crisp, cold air caused a shiver to run up my body as I left the dressmaker's house. It had gotten colder this week out of nowhere, which was odd. We weren't due for cold weather for a few more months; it had come early. I gave one look at the dressmaker's door, debating if I should go in and borrow a coat or just rush to Libby's.

It wouldn't be worth going back in for the coat because then I would run into Mother. So rush to Libby's it was.

I took off in the direction of Libby's house, wrapping my arms around myself, trying to gather some warmth. It wasn't dark yet, but the sun would soon set. A date with Jax later left only a little time to spend with Libby and settle my nerves.

As I made my way through town, I looked around Farplains, the place I'd grown up in. Whoever designed the town had no creativity. The houses were all the same, like they found one design that worked and just reproduced it over and over. It had made sense when wars were a constant thing and buildings got destroyed, but those times were past. Diversifying the homes would do some good, bring a bit more excitement into the town, and draw more business from the other towns. But it would not matter long to me if they implemented change. Once I married Jax, I would move to his town just a day away from home.

Smoke billowed out of the house on my right. The forge next to it allowed Sam to work as a blacksmith without having to leave too far from home—something Libby loved and abused. I took the stairs up to the main house two at a time, and knocked rapidly on the door. The cold was getting to me. When the door creaked open, I did not hesitate to bolt in, not even waiting to be invited, and I almost knocked Sam over .

"Veronica! What are you doing here?" he howled as he tried to get his footing back underneath him.

He might have been a large man, but he was also clumsy. I cast my gaze around, trying to find my intended target, but I could not find Libby.

"Where is Libby?" I asked.

Sam motioned to the back of the house. I turned on my heels and proceeded to the back of the home. Libby was probably in bed. Being pregnant was a new and tiring experience for her. I knocked on the last door in the hallway. As I leaned in to place my ear closer to the door, I waited till her soft voice called out before proceeding in. If she was sleeping, I didn't want to wake her, but luck seemed to be on my side, because she was sitting at her vanity, getting ready for bed.

"You know, it's not even that late and you are acting like an old lady," I said as I plopped down on her bed. I crossed my legs and leveled her with a disappointed stare, which only prompted her to throw her hairbrush at me.

"You try being pregnant!" she exclaimed, laughing.

"It's not on my plan for several years, thank you very much."

"Is something wrong with the dress?"

My nose crinkled. The dress was perfect, or at least I thought it was…

"I don't think Rory likes it…" I muttered.

Libby turned to me, giving me her full attention. She had also noticed the rift between Rory and me. It would have been impossible for her to not notice what was going on between us. Most hadn't picked up on it, but Libby was like another sister to us.

"She has been there every step of the way, physically but not mentally. She is somewhere else, and I'm not sure what to do or what to say to fix things."

"Have you talked to her about it?"

I laughed at that. When had I not tried to talk to her about it? She just shrugged it off, said everything was fine, and disappeared every time. I stared at the ceiling, trying to distract some parts of my mind in hopes I didn't fall down the rabbit hole.

"Let's not ask stupid questions."

"I don't know, Ver, you only have a few days left together. Try to talk to her again before you don't have the chance to anymore."

I covered my face with my hands in frustration as I let out a huge sigh. Only a few days left with Rory, and we would spend it being miserable because she wouldn't open up to me.

"Are you excited about your wedding?" Libby asked, her voice taking on a higher pitch.

I moved my fingers aside so I could crack open an eye at her. With a quick mumble in response, I closed my fingers again, covering my face once more, only for my hands to get pushed aside a moment later as Libby leaned over me.

"You are muffled behind your hands."

"I said yes, I'm excited. I mean, Jax is … nothing special … but it's nice having a celebration."

Libby couldn't contain the laughter that exploded from her. "Is that the only reason you're getting married?"

A smile spread across my face. "Maybe. Who knows?"

My best friend dropped her weight on the bed beside me. Without missing a beat, she snuggled right into my side and spilled everything about the wonders and joys of being married —especially talking about how Sam treated her like a queen and doted on her every waking moment.

I couldn't help but smile. While Jax and I weren't close like Libby and Sam were before their marriage, we could most likely eventually get there, and that was really all one could wish for.

Chapter 2

Leaving Libby's house, curses flew from my mouth as I was once more forced to walk in the cold as I left for my date, but at least Libby had loaned me a jacket to wear. The weather today got biting and ruthless as more time passed. The sun would set soon. I'd spent longer than I should have at Libby's. I was going to be late for my date with Jax.

I wrapped the jacket tighter as I trudged towards the lake. The weather was going to be even colder by the water. I hoped Jax had brought blankets. Another string of curses left my mouth as just thinking about how far the lake was from my house. If it was this cold now, it was going to be unbearable by the time I got home.

One foot in front of the other, my mind wandered as I let muscle memory lead me toward the lake. Libby was great to talk to, but she had provided no tips of usefulness to resolving my relationship with Rory. I snorted. She had spent a great deal of time gushing about how awesome and incredibly handsome Sam was. He was like a little puppy who had fallen in love hard and now wanted to do everything possible to please his love, something that Libby had no problem soaking up.

I took the opportunity when presented to tease him about his behavior, which only caused him to blush and Libby to squeal. I considered them a once-in-a-lifetime couple. What they had wasn't something that could be reproduced easily.

A biting breeze flew in, signaling I was arriving. Jax would be waiting for our date to start. I cast my gaze at the sky. The sun would set soon. My eyes drifted down as I walked the path to the lake, and before me a shadow could be seen, cast in the glow from the setting sun.

And as I got closer, I could tell it was Jax. I let loose a sigh and placed a smile on my face. He didn't make my heart beat wild, didn't capture my breath and make it hard to draw another. No, he was just Jax to me. But soon he'd be my husband, and I hoped one day he'd take my breath away.

Even though he didn't take my breath away, he was still a handsome man. His hair was longer than most men cared to keep it, for it touched the end of his neck and he could tuck the strands that hugged his face behind his ear.

A blanket was spread out, and a basket was placed beside him. The smile on my face got a little less fake and a little more genuine at the gesture. It was a romantic idea, and even though I didn't see Jax as somebody I loved, I hoped we'd get there one day. Just as I approached, he turned to face me, and he shot me a smile, his clean-shaven face on full display. With a gesture he motioned to the empty spot on the blanket beside him, on the other side of the basket.

"Hi," I called out as I finally got close.

His hazel eyes twinkled up at me. His unruly brown hair was tamer today and even slicked back slightly to allow it to stay out of his face. He stood and reached his hand out to me as I stepped on the blanket. As I clasped my hand in his, I could see that his hair looked wet, like he had either just bathed or been for a swim.

He brought my hand up to his lips and placed a quick kiss before letting me sit. It was a gesture that wasn't needed, but I understood. He wanted to be romantic. We were to be husband and wife soon after all.

"Did you go for a swim?" I asked.

He sheepishly rubbed behind his neck. "Heh, you can tell? I needed something to help settle my nerves, so why not take a cold dip?"

He joined me sitting on the blanket. With legs crossed and hands clasped, I waited for him to pull the contents out of the basket. I didn't want to be rude and just assume I could help myself to what lay within. It one of the rare times we were able to hang out alone, away from the watching eyes of the elders. Thought had been put into our date, and I didn't want to look unappreciative for his efforts.

He reached into the basket and pulled out a mixture of meat, cheese, and crackers. The next thing he pulled out of the basket was another container of fruits and veggies. All the contents of the charcuterie spread must not have fit into one.

It was simple food that would be easy to eat at the lake, which was perfect. As he reached back into the basket, my stomach made its presence known. A low rumbling noise broke the silence as I wrapped my arms around my middle to help muffle the noise, but the damage had been done.

Jax laughed as he paused for a moment, grabbing whatever else was in the basket. "Someone is hungry," he said.

The last container held a tray of sweets. From a quick glance, I spotted cookies, muffins, and scones. It seemed Jax knew the secret to my heart already. Sweets were a weakness of mine. He flipped open the side of the basket to retrieve two glasses and a bottle of wine.

"You outdid yourself today," I said as I grabbed the outstretched glass from his hand.

He moved the other glass to his hand holding the bottle before handing me the blanket from the basket. With no time wasted, I unraveled it and I spread it across my legs—another barrier against the cold was greatly appreciated. Jax handed me his glass, and I held them up as he got to work opening the bottle.

"I had a little help," he mumbled as he popped the cork of the wine and poured into our awaiting cups.

"Oh? Who told you all my secrets?" I asked.

I was eager to know who was spilling information about me. I wasn't close to many but I bet he was getting the information from my mother—her way to make sure our match would be perfect so any doubts I had would be settled. I swirled the wine around as I brought it up to my nose for a sniff.

Instantly, I sighed as an earthly aroma with a hint of cherry flooded through my nose. Jax had really done his research on what I would like for tonight's date. He had planned everything perfectly. He finished packaging the wine up so it wouldn't spill while we enjoyed our meal and I handed him his glass. As I brought my glass up to my lips to finally take a sip, he uttered words that froze me.

"Aurora told me," he said.

I watched him from the corner of my eye. With his glass raised, he swirled it only for a moment before taking a long sip. Rory had been the one to tell Jax about the things I liked? If it was Libby or Mother, that was one thing, but that my sister spilled information about me so easily but yet could not speak *to* me. Pain stabbed at my heart.

Did she just feel more comfortable talking to Jax? Confusion bubbled in my head. I'd been trying to spend time with her before she left, but she'd been spending time with Jax, and I didn't even know it! If anything, the three of us could have just hung out, but I was left out, and I wanted to know why.

"That's odd ... Rory has been different lately," I said as Jax brought his glass to his lips once more, letting it linger there for a few moments after his sip. He was avoiding something, and I was tired of people avoiding me. Why did everyone else seem to know what was going on except me?

"Yeah…" Jax mumbled.

"You know what's going on, don't you?" My tone was harsh, but I didn't care.

People were keeping secrets from me that involved my sister. Future husband be damned, I wasn't going to let another person stand in the way of our relationship.

"It needs to be handled between sisters. You need to talk to Aurora."

"You don't think I've tried?" I exclaimed. "Do you think I like being ignored by my little sister?"

I could feel my anger rising. For him to tell me to talk to my sister … as if that wasn't obvious … that was what I had been trying to do all along! I didn't want to force her to talk, but now knowing she was spilling everything to Jax hurt. The anger was morphing into pain. All I wanted was to be close, to spend our last days together happy before we were forced to part. I wasn't sure when we'd be able to see each other again—if ever—so I wanted our last memories to be filled with happiness. But instead it was sadness.

"What's so special about you that she can open up to you and not me?" I quietly asked as I stared at the ground.

"Like I said, Veronica, this needs to be handled between sisters."

My hand balled into a fist before unclenching and yanking my blanket off. I brought the glass to my lips and downed the rest of the wine. It would help numb my aching heart. As soon as I stood up, I whirled on Jax and stared him in the eyes.

"Let's go, then. We're going to find Rory right now." I reached down to grab hold of his arm to tug him along. I wasn't sure where we 'd find Rory, but I was determined. And when one was determined, things would fall into place.

"We can't leave now. The elders are expecting us to be on a date. It wouldn't look good for either one of us if we showed up so early."

I stared at him, mulling over his words. He was correct. If we showed up back in town so soon, we'd be bombarded by the elders and certainly Mother. As the only wedding happening this month, and the only one to happen for the next several months, it was a big deal in the town. Everyone wanted this to go smoothly. It wasn't every day the leader's daughter married.

They would consume our time trying to figure out what happened, and I wouldn't be able to seek out Rory for answers. No, if I wanted answers tonight, then I'd at least have to wait till later in the night.

I bit my lip in frustration at being thwarted on getting answers from my sister. I wanted things resolved. I just wanted my relationship with my sister to be back to normal. I let out a sigh as I picked at the spread of food.

There would be no more talking between Jax and me. The mood was ruined. Instead of opting to fill my glass with more wine, I grabbed the bottle and drank straight from it. If I was going to be forced to sit here and not fix my relationship with my sister, at least I'd do it my way.

Chapter 3

I was numb, not only mentally, but physically. The silence between Jax and I had been deafening, and I couldn't handle it anymore. He understood and respected my wishes. We only made it an hour from our discussion before I asked him to leave. Every time I looked at him, all I could see was Rory spilling her heart out to him and refusing to say anything to me. The majority of the town would be asleep now, or at the tavern getting drunk. He promised to stay hidden so people wouldn't notice him walking about in town. We still didn't need people sticking their noses into our business when everything was falling apart.

I wrapped the blanket even tighter against my body, trying to calm the shivers. After he left, a walk was my first attempt to cool my mind, but it didn't work. Instead, I opted to jump into the freezing water. It provided the shock I needed, but now I had to walk home wet, in the cold. Maybe if I got sick we could delay the wedding, which would delay Rory's departure. But that was only a pipe dream.

I sneezed, my chest tightening in the process. There was a high chance I was going to get sick. Sighing, I tried to bury myself deeper into my blanket. Darkness had fallen. I had wanted to talk to Rory hours ago, but this was my time to finally get answers on what was going on.

What had caused the rift between us?

Jax had left the basket in case I got hungry. That would have normally put a smile on my face for him being so considerate, but all I could muster was a frown. It was hard to think of Jax as my future husband, because right now he was my sister's secret-keeper. The feelings that rushed through my body were overwhelming. I ground my teeth, body tensing as the feeling of worthless and dread flooded through my body. It was a mixed bag of everything under the sun, and it was just too much.

Instead of dwelling on my sister's situation or the increasing darkness around me, I focused on the path ahead. The trees started to thin out as I grew closer to the cluster of businesses and homes that made up the center of the town. The lights in some of the homes illuminated the path as they shone onto the street. But it was only a house every so often.

People were already falling asleep. I took in my surroundings to see just how far away from home I was. Instantly my eyes landed on the lone tavern of the town. Just by it would be the inn and barn, which meant I'd be home very soon.

Before I could focus back on the path ahead, something shifted by the tavern door. More like three things shifted. My breath hitched as one of the shadows leaning against the walls stood and walked toward the light. A whistle pierced the air and I gripped the basket tighter in my hands. I could fight, and he had another thing coming for him if he thought I was easy prey. I never stopped walking, and kept my peripheral vision trained on the men.

"Another pretty lady tonight, eh? What did we do to get so lucky?" the man said as he stepped into the light. He was a burly man, while his friend behind him seemed to have a slim frame. The man who spoke didn't have a single hair on the top of his head, but his friend had too much, to the point it was unruly. But he did have a beard.

"Spare a few minutes, darling? We can make it quick," the man said, followed up by a chuckle, but I did my best to show I wasn't listening.

I certainly wasn't interested.

"Idiots, that's Veronica." The man that spoke this time had a soothing voice, causing me to turn and look.

I squinted, trying to make out the crouched figure in the shadows. But the tavern was doing a good job of hiding him from sight. He shifted; the light illuminated his silver hair and his equally silver eyes. Pools of silver stared straight into my soul, causing me to stop walking and fully turn to look at the man.

Silver hair with silver eyes were not a common trait in the village. If he was someone who lived here, I would have certainly noticed him before. The longer he stared into my soul, the more the tingle in the back of my mind grew. It took a moment for realization to settle before I truly understood what was happening. The tingle was a warning, kicking off the flight or fight response. But I was frozen, staring into the silver pools of his eyes.

The man leaned forward, his mouth curving as his lips parted. Alarms were blaring as his incredible white teeth shone in the night. While that would have been a beautiful sight, it was the pair of sharpened teeth in his mouth that was causing everything to go crazy inside.

"Vampire..." I whispered.

His mouth quickly closed, hiding his teeth as he leaned back into the shadows. Had he heard me?

"Just our luck! First Aurora and now Veronica. Where are the regular ladies? I'm not trying to get my hand chopped off," the bald man grumbled as his friend nodded eagerly. The alarms were silenced immediately as I processed his words.

"You saw Aurora recently?" I asked. Why was she out so late and where did she go? There would be no point in going home to talk to her if she wasn't even there.

"Lost sight of the princess or something?" the bald man said once more, then he turned his attention back to me.

"What do you have to trade for the information?" the skinny man asked as he made his way closer to me, his hands reaching out with every step.

Instinctively, I brought the basket up and chucked it at the man. Considering the fact the basket still had the contents from the picnic in it, it packed quite a punch when it hit him squarely in his head.

My nose crinkled as I took in the view of him sprawled out on the ground. The second he'd stepped too close, I could tell he was drunk. With the alcohol in his system, there was a good chance he'd be sleeping in the street tonight. That was, if his friend didn't drag him to the inn. I shifted my attention to the man who was still standing.

"Hey! What was that for? He was just trying to talk!" the man shouted, and I scoffed. His definition of talk was definitely different from mine.

He inched his way toward me, and I steeled myself for a fight.

"Stop," the silver-haired man said as he got up from his position.

Still enclosed slightly in the shadows, he turned toward the tavern door and opened it. The noise inside blasted out.

"Get inside, idiot," he muttered.

The idiot lingered for a moment before entering the tavern, which left me in the streets with one unconscious drunk and one silver-haired man in the doorway.

"She's at the stables."

A smile spread across my face. I'd gotten the information and now all I needed to do was finally talk to Rory and settle things between us so everything could go back to normal.

"Thanks!" I shouted as I turned to head to the barn.

"I wouldn't go if I was you…" he drawled as he looked over his shoulder at me, the silver pools of his eyes once more captivating me.

But only for a moment. I had waited all day—actually, several days—to talk to Rory, and the knowledge that she'd spilled everything to my soon-to-be husband sent pangs through my heart. Whatever had caused this rift between us needed to be settled, and I wouldn't let the advice of a man I didn't know deter me. I was going to fix whatever was wrong between Rory and me tonight. And that was final.

CHAPTER 4

I t wasn't the brightest idea to listen to the man with silver hair, but out of the group he seemed the most likely to provide accurate information. It might just have been desperation at wanting to have a chance to mend things between my sister and I before we lost the chance. I didn't want my last week with her to be filled with memories of us barely talking. We were inseparable growing up, and now there was a whole world between us.

The stable door was only a half door, which made it easy to peer into as I approached the building. It was dark inside, and I could see the horses shuffling in their enclosures, but no human in sight. The equipment for the animals was located up front, and that area was empty. If she wasn't at the barn, was she at home? The burly man had said he came across Aurora, and the silver-haired man had said she was here. So they must have crossed her at some point.

The wind picked up as it slammed against the blanket. Not having to hold the basket allowed me to have my hands tucked away from the wind, but a shiver coursed through my body. I needed to head home—enough time had already been spent outside acting a fool.

I turned back to the street, but paused as a laugh echoed in the air. A very familiar laugh, one I 'd not heard for a while for the owner of the voice was avoiding me. Hope surged inside; Rory was still out here and she was in a good mood! Maybe we could finally figure this out and get things back to normal. The laugh broke the silence of the night once more as I peered around the side of the barn. She wasn't in the barn but behind it. Why?

Rory's voice filled the air once more, a bit muffled, but I knew it was her as I made my way to the back of the barn, her voice increasing in volume with every step I took. She wasn't alone. There was someone with her—she was talking. My movement stopped as she spoke my name, followed by some hushed words. She was talking about me to someone. Pain tugged at my heart. She was telling everyone else her problems instead of me.

I proceeded forward, the end of the barn in sight, but I wasn't sure of what I should do. With her talking to someone else about me, I would look suspicious, like I'd been spying, which could drive an even bigger wedge between us.

Everyone would soon be asleep and the dwellers in the tavern would be heading home. I couldn't linger out here too long unless I wanted to cross paths with some drunken men again.

There wouldn't always be a silver-haired man in each group to keep a leash on the company he kept. With a new resolve to not spend all night out here, I'd first see who Rory was talking to. Hopefully not someone important.

With a step forward, my heart shattered as my little sister's sobs filled the air. Something had changed in the short window of when I first heard her. I continued my approach, dreading what was around the corner.

She was broken, spilling her feelings out to someone, and I didn't know who. The only thing I did know was that she felt more comfortable with them than I.

If it were possible for my shattered heart to break into more pieces, it did, for a new voice joined the sobs of my sister, paralyzing everything in my body as I couldn't process what was happening. A voice I'd heard just mere hours ago was here behind the barn with my sister in the dead of night, discussing me.

He spoke calming words, trying to soothe my sister. I continued almost in a daze as I made it to the back of the barn, not daring to peek around for it would just make everything real. If I didn't see it, then maybe it would all be a dream. None of this could be real. But I needed the proof. He'd said it needed to be handled between sisters, but he never mentioned how big his role was in our issue. I crouched close to the ground as I slowly poked my head around the corner, doing my best to not expose myself. If I saw who I thought the voice belonged to, there would be no way I could approach them. Not in the dead of night like this.

My eyes instantly zeroed in on the embrace, the way his arms wrapped low around her waist, her face to his chest as she gripped his shirt. Her sobs were slowing down. He had successfully soothed her, but in doing so he'd shattered everything between us. His long brown hair blew softly in the wind as he unwrapped one arm from my sister's waist to tuck a strand behind his ear before returning his arm to her waist. A smile spread across his face, and a frown spread across mine as my sister shifted to look up at him.

"I wish we could be together."

My hands rushed to clamp over my mouth, muffling the gasp that wanted to escape. He leaned down and placed a quick kiss on Rory's head. If it was anyone else she was with, I would have been happy—would have teased her about it, but would definitely be ecstatic for her.

But it wasn't just anybody. She had her arms around Jax in a loving embrace. My future husband.

I tucked back behind the barn, trying to calm my rapidly beating heart, to soothe the panic that was threating to take over.

Rory was to leave soon, to go live with the vampires, which would leave me behind with Jax. But how could I marry him, even move to his village, knowing he loved my sister? Maybe if he had fallen in love with another girl, someone not my sister, I would have been able to look past it. But knowing that he would be looking at me and wishing it was my sister was too much to ask me to bear.

Rory's voice cracked as she spoke: "Could we run away together? I want to be with you."

Knowing the true cause of the rift between us, I crashed backward, landing on my butt, my hands digging into the dirt, doing my best to not have my face meet the ground as well. My arms felt like jelly; I shook, and it wasn't because the night was cold. No, I was frozen inside at the realization of my sister and Jax being in love. She wanted to run away together, but would she have confessed to me what was truly going on?

I might have handled things better if she'd come to me, but finding out like this would shatter anyone's soul. Everything was just a twisted joke, and it was making me sick.

I wanted to leave, but my body and mind were separate, no longer functioning together, as my mind was breaking into pieces.

"We can't. Where would we go?"

Rory's sobs started up once more at having her dreams dashed, unable to handle the reality of the situation.

"I'm scared. I don't think I can handle being away from you," she said.

I heaved. It was a tragic love story, and I was the one driving the wedge between them. Without me, they could live happily ever after. But things were already set in motion and couldn't be undone.

Betrayal, hurt—a thousand other emotions—were swarming inside, and soon they would erupt, unable to be suppressed. Was I even on her mind the past few weeks of us not talking? She was always at the forefront of my mind. We were sisters. We should have had an unshakable bond—the way we used to have —but it all changed when Jax came into the picture.

She was my sister, my best friend, and my partner in crime, but the girl in a loving embrace with my future husband was not the same girl I knew. This one kept secrets, devastating ones that would shatter my world if they ever came to light. Maybe that was her way of protecting me—if I didn't know of it, what harm could it do if she kept me in the dark?

But the darkness didn't agree, for it was a creature of night that had led me to her.

Although he had said I shouldn't go, but I didn't listen.

No one was talking anymore. The only thing I could hear was the voice in my head trying to process everything. Against all better judgment, I maneuvered myself once more to see if they were behind the barn. But I wished I hadn't.

He had his lips to hers in a heated display of affection, something never shared between us. Her hands came to rest in his hair as he slid his hands higher up her back, closing any sort of distance between them that might have existed.

Tears welled inside and I had no energy to hold them back. There would be no point. I could never be Jax's wife and Rory's sister.

I wanted to cry out, but that would let them know I was here. There was only so much heartbreak a girl could handle in one night, and I'd received my fill and so much more. For each gasp of air they took, it drove a knife deeper into my heart. They may have not stuck with me with a real blade but the fire spreading through my body was real. Scorching my heart with every word uttered, ignited by the betrayal of my sister and husband to be.

"Will you walk me back?" Rory asked as they finally broke their loving embrace.

Panic flooded me as they broke apart holding hands. I couldn't be caught out here spying on them. My feet carried me straight to the front of the barn and over the doors, straight into one of the horses' pens. It was safer to hide out than head home, because we'd have to take the same path. They would eventually see me.

Giggles erupted and filled the air, spiking my curiosity. I peered out from my hiding position. Rory ran in front of the barn, but Jax was fast as he caught her arm. He twirled her around and straight into his embrace as he swayed back and forth. Their loving embrace glowed under the moonlight, casting an image that would forever be burned in my mind. She pushed off of Jax as she took off running, him following, both of them laughing. Their voices got harder to hear as they made their way away from the barn, unknown to them that I was falling to pieces inside.

It took a while to urge my body from the hiding spot. If I stayed for much longer, I would see the sunrise with the company of horses. The scent of the horses lingered on my skin. I'd need a bath when I got home—a blistering hot bath that I'd be too numb to feel.

The path home was a familiar one that I'd walked many times before. But tonight, the only thing I could see was Rory laughing while being chased by Jax.

Movement at the corner of my eye caught my attention, and I stopped.

Silver eyes stared at me in the dark. I stared back. How long had he been out here, and had he seen everything as well? It seemed it wasn't enough to drive a knife through my heart at the revelation of my sister and Jax being in love, but having an audience was just cruel. It might have only been one person watching, but it was one too many.

I made my way home once more, ignoring the silver eyes boring into my back, sending a hint of a tingle through my numb body. But it wasn't enough to draw me from my haze. All I wanted and all I needed was for this night to end.

CHAPTER 5

The ceiling became the highlight of my days but also the bane of my existence. It acted as a blank canvas, allowing me to project my thoughts on it, bringing my memories to life. It allowed me to watch memories of when I was happy, of when Rory and I had an unbreakable bond.

But with every thought of my sister, my mind drifted back to the events at the barn that night. It had been several days but the memory was just as vivid, burning at the forefront of my mind. Everything had gone by the wayside. A true mess had been created, and I was left standing in it with no idea of how to fix anything. Was it even something that could be fixed?

I grabbed hold of the blanket bunched up around my waist and threw it over my head, curling up into a ball. I'd spent days in my bedroom refusing to leave, partly due to being sick but mostly due to not wanting to face the world. Because of that, my wedding was tomorrow and it would also be the last day I would see Rory. She'd be sent to the vampires as an offering, and I'd be left with the knowledge that my husband could never love me.

Mother had let me waste away in my room, but that would not hold true for today. Preparations needed to be done, and they couldn't be finalized if the wife-to-be wasn't present. I would have to emerge back into the world today, regardless of whether I was ready to or not.

A light knock against my door chimed through the quiet room. I grabbed my pillow to cover my face. If I didn't acknowledge it, would the person go away?

But the knocking didn't stop, it only increased. I was afraid that if they continued, I would have a door no longer, and then I would truly have no way to hide from the world. With reluctance, I threw the pillow off my face, got out of bed, and headed to the door.

My body groaned at the movement. Being bedridden had taken its toll. I could only hope that whoever was banging on my door had a good reason for doing so or they would receive a door in the face when I closed it and went back to bed.

The sting of annoyance shifted into one of concern as my best friend stared back at me.. Her long blond hair was braided out of her face, and her gray eyes shone with joy at seeing me. She shoved a basket in my direction as she pushed into the room.

"Libby … what are you doing here?" I asked, as I closed the door behind her.

"I brought gifts!" she exclaimed as she wobbled over to the table. She was several months pregnant, her belly so swollen so it had me thinking there was a chance there would be more than one baby.

"It's not really the best time right now…"

"You aren't even doing anything. Come!" she said as she patted the table, wanting me to join her as opened up her basket with a smile still on her face.

I watched her as she messed with the items she had brought. There was no way I could kick her out. She knew I had a soft spot for her in my heart. Her hands were busy at work, grabbing the contents from the basket as I pulled out a chair and joined her.

A delicious and very sweet aroma hit me as she brought out something wrapped in a deep red cloth. Maybe it was a good thing I hadn't turned her away.

"What did you bring?" I asked as I reached for the red cloth, but she quickly smacked my hand away.

"So it's a good time now, huh?" There was a mischievous smirk on her face.

I rested my elbow on the table and my head on my hand as I stared at her, not amused at all.

"All right, all right! If looks could kill, I would be six feet in the ground," she said, followed by a laugh as she grabbed the white cloth package, the very first package removed from the basket, and unwrapped it.

"Cheese and bread?" I asked, raising my eyebrow . That wasn't much of a gift. They were common items in every kitchen.

"Sorry! That's actually for me," she said sheepishly as she pushed the blue cloth package my way.

She happily plucked away at her snack as my fingers got to work unwrapping the blue cloth.

"If it's more food..." I started as I undid the final knot, allowing the cloth to fall to the side. But instead of food, it was a piece of jewelry.

"For your wedding. I thought it would go nicely with your dress," she uttered softly.

I leaned over the table and placed a quick kiss on her cheek in thanks. I wasn't much of a jewelry person, opting to not buy pieces for myself, but I loved to receive pieces from others because they must have been thinking about me when they picked them out, and that caused me to smile.

The largest item wrapped in the cloth was a silver hairpiece with prongs, an accessory decorated with flowers not local to our area, something that would have cost Libby a pretty penny to acquire. The centerpiece of the hair accessory had blue petals carefully laid out, overlapping, giving the illusion it was one big flower, but it was several small flowers put together. Faded leaves decorated behind the flowers, allowing the blue tint of the petals to stand out even more. But that wasn't all, because once the flower was complete, there were three strands that dangled down. Additional flowers were scattered down the chains till they stopped at a mix of a yellow and orange stone.

"Forget-me-nots and citrine quartz."

"It's beautiful," I mumbled, dazed at the craftsmanship on the jewelry. This wasn't a common piece that could just be found anywhere. This had to be a custom request.

"I know you don't like to wear jewelry, but I figured you'd make an exception."

Indeed, she was right. Jewelry was a luxury most girls had no problems partaking in, but I didn't have that same desire. But it was a gift from Libby with meaning, so of course I would make an exception for her.

With the hairpiece safely wrapped back up in the blue cloth, I reached for the package wrapped in a silver cloth. Immediately upon picking it up, I knew what it would be, for it was something I was familiar with. Unwrapping the thread that wound around the silver cloth, a smile spread across my face. If Mother had been here, she would have a fit and demanded Libby take the gift away.

Girls were meant to be delicate, and a dagger was the exact opposite of it. A basic brown leather scabbard was the first thing I wrapped my fingers around as I examined the weapon. From the outside, it looked simple, but I tugged at the dagger, removing it from its sheath, and it told a different story.

An appreciative whistle escaped my lips. Libby had gone all out when producing my wedding gifts. The flower hairpiece was marvelous, a beauty in itself, but this dagger? It was as if it wasn't of this world. The handle on the dagger was silver wrapped in black leather straps. But it was the blade that was breathtakingly beautiful. It was a dark gray, with intricate swirls throughout.

If Libby wasn't already one of my favorite people in this world, then this would have sealed the deal, for she had gifted me a Damascus steel dagger. It was a blade of the night. It wasn't flashy and bright like the daggers that drew attention. This dagger was something someone would use in the dead of night; the darkness of the steel would conceal it till it was too late.

"Odd choice for a dagger, but, Libby, you have outdone yourself!" I exclaimed as I swung the dagger lightly, getting a feel for it.

"Do you like it?"

"Do I like it? That is an understatement. I love it!"

"I'm glad! The shop owner who helped me out insisted I take this blade and wouldn't let me purchase any other one. I was slightly worried you might not like it…"

"What an odd person, but I am glad she gave you this."

Libby nodded along as she reached once more to her white cloth that protected her cheese and crackers and started nibbling away.

I placed the dagger back in the scabbard as I reached for the last package on the table—the deep red cloth that contained the wonderful aroma. My mouth watered as I hastily broke away the cloth to get to its center. My eyes landed on the chocolatey goodness and I smiled.

Libby was definitely my favorite person in this entire world. The chocolate was hard, but bark was supposed to be. I shoved a piece into my mouth, a loud crack echoing in the room. I paused briefly as the flavors came to life, sending a shiver of delight down my spine. Oh, it was good. Very good. I shoved the rest of the bark into my mouth as I reached for another, but Libby smacked my hand away.

"It's for tomorrow."

"But it's fig chocolate!" I exclaimed as I reached for the pieces once more, but Libby was a mother bear protecting her cubs. She wrapped the contents back in the red cloth quickly and pushed it out of reach from my grabby hands.

Fig chocolate was a treat we didn't eat often in the town. It wasn't that chocolate was rare per se, but everyone preferred its softer form of cake. As one of the very few people who preferred the hardness of bark, I always lost when it came to how we should use our chocolate. Bark was more practical than chocolate cake—one didn't have to worry about it morphing into a pile of goop if not packaged properly.

"I got extra for you as well!" Libby exclaimed happily as she clapped her hands.

"So let me eat some now, then!" I whined in response.

Why was she teasing me so? If there was extra fig chocolate, then I should be allowed to eat my fill.

"I heard it's supposed to give you an extra kick if you know what I mean," Libby said as she wiggled her eyebrows at me.

An extra kick? Realization dawned on me as I knew what she was trying to say. It was something I should consume on my wedding day so I would have the extra kick for when night rolled around. But instead of being happy like she was, I was filled with dread. With Libby's presence and the unwrapping of gifts, I had forgotten about who exactly I was to marry tomorrow. When I thought of my soon-to-be husband, I thought of my Rory. Them in a loving embrace, sharing a passionate kiss under the moonlight.

My gaze drifted to the chocolate wrapped away safely in the red cloth. And now I would be expected to lie with him to consummate our marriage, but would he be thinking of me ... or would he be thinking of Rory?

I groaned in frustration as I started to feel sick all over again. The image of them locking in an embrace, of them laughing and chasing one another, of their lips pressed together…

I dug my fingers into my hair, gripping tightly, shaking my head vigorously, trying to cast the images from my mind, but it continued to replay on repeat.

Defeated, I allowed my head to fall and smack into the table. The short burst of pain when my head met the wood was enough to stop the thoughts, but only for a moment. So I did what any sane girl would do when they found a way to stop the replay of memories—I continued to bang my head against the table.

"What are you doing?" Libby asked, concerned. She placed her hands on the table, stopping me from continuing the assault on my forehead.

"Everything is a mess," I croaked out as I leaned forward, fully intent on smacking my head into the table again, but Libby would have none of it. She dug her fingernails into my temple, causing me to screech as I jerked my head away from her.

"What was that for?" I screamed as I rubbed my forehead, wondering if her nails had left a bruise.

"Did that one piece of chocolate make you go crazy?"

I stared into her eyes. I could tell she was concerned, but I couldn't spill the events of that night to her. It would worry her too much, and I didn't want her to bear it. She had enough to deal with being pregnant, most likely with two, my move away after the wedding, and the rift between Rory and I. She was sure it was something that could be repaired and we would be back to normal, but I wasn't convinced. My sister was set to leave tomorrow, and I was set to marry the man she'd fallen in love with.

"Do you have doubts about your wedding?" Libby asked.

I wanted to snort. I had doubts, that was for sure. But everything was set in stone. The vampires would take Rory away, and I would marry Jax. A wedding was to take place tomorrow.

"What happens if I don't go through with the wedding?" I whispered.

"What do you mean?"

"Like cancel the wedding."

"Someone has to get married. Vampires will be here to collect the offering."

I sighed. I already knew deep down that the wedding couldn't be canceled, but there was something calming about hearing it from another person. As if it told me I wasn't crazy.

But it didn't make my situation better. It just sealed it.

"Everyone has moments of doubt. It would be weird if you didn't. Your whole life is about to change," Libby said softly as she maneuvered out of her seat to come sit beside me.

Instead of smacking my head into the table in an attempt to smother the memories, I opted to just rest my head on Libby's chest as she wrapped her arms around me. She ran her fingers through my hair, rocking from side to side.

"Do you know what happens to someone once they're offered?" I questioned.

I needed something to distract my mind from the passionate kiss shared between Rory and Jax.

"Supposedly, they live like royalty with the vampires till their death. But it's mostly rumors. Once people are offered, we don't really see them again. Why waste time traveling to a town that never changes when there is a whole world out there ready to be explored?" I didn't respond, just opting to listen to her heartbeat.

"You should talk to Rory about it. She has spent way more time learning about vampires than either of us."

My body stiffened against her, causing her rocking to stop. Her fingers no longer ran through my hair as she pushed me up so she could look into my eyes.

"You didn't resolve the issue with Rory yet? You have been home for days! What have you been doing?"

"Sleeping?" I sheepishly replied.

She had to have spent time outside the village picking up my wedding gifts, so she must not have caught wind that I had locked myself up in my room, refusing to leave, with what most thought was a bug that would pass…

"I'm a bit tired…" I whispered as I slowly stepped away from the table and in the direction of my bed.

But Libby didn't agree. Her hand clamped on my ear, twisting her fingers and yanking me in the direction of the door.

"All right, all right! I will go talk to Rory! Just let go!" I whined.

She let go of her hold as I opened the door and looked into her eyes, waiting for her to leave, but she didn't move.

"Aren't you going to leave?" I asked.

"Oh, I'm staying. You are the one leaving," she said as she pushed me out of my own bedroom, slamming the door behind me.

I grasped the doorknob and jiggled it. She was a speedy one. She had already locked the door before I could react. I sighed at her antics. She'd left me no choice but to find Rory now. Why did I have such a troublesome life?

Chapter 6

It had been several hours since Libby had locked me out of my room and still no Rory in sight. But I wasn't really trying to find her, for I didn't know what to say. Was I supposed to say I saw her behind the barn kissing my future husband, where she asked him to run away.

Were you ever going to tell me?

I scoffed. Yeah that wasn't something I wanted to talk about. Instead of focusing on my sister, I opted to take in home. My days here were limited. Once I became a married woman, I would be expected to move to the village where my husband resided.

People moved with pep in their step. There was still a bunch to do in preparation for the wedding. Only a few people stopped to say hello. Most opted to ignore me and continue with their business. I couldn't blame them. I probably looked like the walking dead. Being locked in my room for several days, trying to process that my life would never be the same, took its toll.

Tonight would be a celebration for the one who would be offered. Then tomorrow would be the wedding, followed by seeing off the offering to the vampires, and finally the night would end in another celebration. But the thought of all the events that should have brought a smile to my face only made me frown. It was a reminder of the ticking clock between Rory, Jax, and me. Once the vows were exchanged between Jax and me, all three of our fates would be sealed, and I wasn't sure if anyone would win in the end. I certainly wouldn't.

The town was starting to get overwhelming as more people got to work setting up for the dance tonight. All I wanted was some peace and quiet, and without thinking my feet moved on their own, answering my prayers. I made my way toward the lake. It was where Jax and I went on our date, but that was a sliver of the memories I had of the lake.

There was a reason we had our date there—it was one of my favorite spots in the town. It had been my spot long before the night of the date, and it would continue to be my spot long afterward. That was something I was sure of.

All the walking around town had left me close to my safe haven, and I wasted no time stripping off my garments, leaving me in nothing but my birthday suit as I walked straight into the water. The coldness bit at my skin, but only briefly, as I adjusted with every step.

Everyone would be too busy dealing with party setup; it would allow me to have a nice swim before I had to face reality. With a deep breath, I fully submerged myself underwater, letting the lake do its wonders, caressing me in its embrace, shifting me slowly with the flow of the water. Submerged in the darkness, I allowed calm to take hold.

It was a different world down here. It provided an escape from the world above bearing down on my shoulders, waiting for me to deal with it. The allure of the living world was too much; pain throbbed in my throat. I needed air if I wanted to stay part of the world above.

I kicked my legs, bringing myself back to the surface for a huge breath, calming the pain in my throat. When the pain disappeared, I prepared to take another big breath for another dive, but the cracking of branches paused my descent.

Everyone should be busy with the dance tonight.

But I was wrong. I wasn't alone. Someone was standing in the trees surrounding the lake.

But no one emerged and no further noise reached my ears.

Had they left? With another big breath, I dipped into the water, hiding myself from sight. I didn't stay as long. I didn't want to experience that burning sensation again, so I broke the surface once more. This time, though, I saw a figure leaning against a tree, arms crossed against his chest as his silver eyes bored into me, as if he was trying to read my soul.

I motioned to him, beckoning him to join me in the water, but he didn't move. Did vampires even know how to swim? I pushed forward, bringing myself closer to him, but still safely in the water, allowing me to have a better view of him. Those silver eyes tracked my every movement.

The night we met, the only things I was able to see were his silver hair, his equally silver eyes, and a brief glance at the sharpened fangs in his mouth. But in broad daylight I could see every inch of him. His hair was slick straight. It reached just a little past his shoulders. Jax had kept his hair long, but it was nothing compared to the man leaning against the tree, watching me. The right side was tucked behind his ear, while the left side softly flowed in the wind, covering his eye from time to time.

If I stood beside him, he would only be a head taller than I. But to confirm it I would need to leave the water. That made my nakedness pop back into my mind.

He was a retriever. It was my first time seeing a retriever out in the open during the day. I had caught a glance of the one who came for Libby's sister, but he'd worn a cloak and didn't mingle with us humans.

This one was different. He was at the tavern that night. He didn't keep the best of company, but he mingled with humans.

The longer I stared at him, the more I was compelled to find out more about the ones sent to pick up the offerings, often opting to only being addressed by their title. Would he share his name if I asked?

He pushed off the tree, standing tall, his eyes never leaving mine. He wore dark trousers with high boots that were great for riding. His long-sleeved black shirt billowed in the wind, a size too big. But it did little to cover his chest, exposed by the dipping V-neck of his shirt. A glint on his chest caught my attention as he was wearing a silver chain.

I kicked my feet, inching closer to the side of the lake where he stood. A slew of cracking branches behind me jerked my attention away from the silver retriever to see who else was joining us at the lake. But no one emerged immediately, although the cracking of branches was getting louder. I turned back to the silver-haired man, intent on learning more about him, but the spot where he once stood was no longer occupied.

A groan escaped me as I took a deep breath and dunked myself underwater once more. Instead of being forced to replay the dreaded night I'd experienced several days ago, the images of Jax and Rory were replaced by the silver man. The way his eyes bored into mine, his hair flowing in the wind. It was an image that provided a good distraction.

The tingle in my throat was back as I emerged above the water once more. For good measure, I looked at the spot where the silver-haired man once stood to see if he had returned, but he hadn't. Instead, I turned to look in the other direction.

Light brown hair was the first thing I picked out as the person made their way closer to the lake. As I squinted to get a better look, my heart froze. Adrenaline shot through my body, my mouth opening in response but causing me to swallow a mouthful of water. A choked cry escaped as I coughed out what I could.

I needed to hide, but being in the middle of the lake made my options limited. I took in a huge breath, throat already burning from swallowing a mouthful just moments ago, then ducked under the water. But the burn was too intense, and I shot straight out of the water, inhaling as much air as I could.

My timing was horrible. I locked eyes with Rory, staring at me from the shore. She paused briefly before continuing closer to stand at the edge of the water. There would be no hiding from her now. I couldn't delay this confrontation anymore.

There was a time I would have done anything to fix the rift between us—only days ago— but it felt like a lifetime. Now, given the opportunity to talk to her, I wasn't sure what I was supposed to say. Was there even anything for me *to* say?

She hesitantly raised her hand and waved. What was a girl supposed to do?

The only thing that would delay the inevitable—hide once more.

I gasped, inhaling as I sank underwater, trying to hide from my worries. Instead, the water was betraying me. My throat stung. The time I was able to stay underwater was getting shorter and shorter. Soon I would have to leave the water or it would claim me. I bobbed my head back above water.

Rory beckoned me to shore. My legs kicked forward. I could not delay it anymore. We didn't even have twenty-four hours together anymore. We would be separated and never see each other again. If we wanted to resolve the rift between us, it had to be now.

She reached into the bag that was on her shoulder and pulled out a blanket, before dipping her feet in the water to meet my arrival. Her outstretched arms wrapped the blanket around my body as I emerged from the water, the cold air only having a brief moment to bite against my skin before the warmth of the blanket took over.

"Hey…" she muttered.

I responded with my own quiet greeting as I followed behind her, the awkwardness between us growing with every step as we made our way to my discarded clothes. There would be no point getting dressed immediately unless I wanted to return to town in wet clothes.

No, I was stuck wrapped in a blanket for at least several minutes, time I would have to spend with Rory, and there was only one thing on both of our minds. I was sure of it.

"So you were looking for me?" she asked, her gaze locked on the water.

"I was…"

"I ran into Libby, and she was very concerned about you. Practically begged me to come find you," she said once more.

Her words were like daggers. She hadn't sought me out because she wanted to. It wasn't her that wanted to mend the broken bond between us. It was Libby. I let out a sigh. Was our relationship really that doomed? If that was the case, it was best to rip the Bandage right off. It would only hurt one of us after all.

"Rory…" I stared at my sister, who refused to look my way, still watching the water. "What is going on between us?"

"I'm just going through things," she whispered, her arms coming to wrap around her legs, bringing them to her chest.

"Talk to me about it," I urged. But she was silent.

She wouldn't spill, so off came the Band-Aid.

"I know … about you and Jax." This time it was me not able to look at her. I kept my gaze trained on the lake, but I could still see her from the corner of my eye.

She had whipped her head around to stare at me, her eyes wide. "How? I wanted to tell you but I didn't know how," she said as she brought her hand to my shoulder.

I turned to her, tears flowing down my cheeks. "You should have told me. I shouldn't have found out the way I did." The pang in my chest was heavy, and having her by my side made it worse.

"How?" she whispered.

"I saw you the night behind the barn."

She gasped; her hand flew from my shoulder to her mouth to try and muffle the additional noise that threatened to spill.

I wasn't in love with Jax, but I would be expected to be. We would be pushed to have children and I would have to wear a mask that conveyed we were a happily married couple, but how could I knowing that when he looked at me he was probably thinking of Rory? Even when I looked at him, all I would be reminded of was that he was my younger sister's love, and of the night at the barn.

"Oh gosh. I'm the absolute worst sister. Veronica, I'm so sorry! I never meant to hurt you." Tears wet her cheeks as she spilled her feelings to me.

If only she had been up front and honest with me days ago instead of the day before my wedding.

"There is just so much going on! Growing up, all I ever wanted to do was explore the world, see what it had to offer, but when Jax came to meet you for the first time, things changed. I didn't want to explore the world anymore, I just wanted to be by his side."

My heart was already aching, but knowing for Rory that it was love at first sight was something hard to process. Was it love at first sight for Jax as well? They'd not said anything, letting me proceed with the wedding. The whole reason I was to be wed in the first place was to allow Rory to be an offering, so she could live her dream. I thought I was a good sister, but instead I'd shattered both of our dreams.

"Veronica, I'm sorry. I never planned on it. But one thing led to another, and then we were in far too deep to turn back…"

I stared at my younger sister. Could she also tell it hurt me that she kept this secret from me for so long? I pushed off the ground, dropping the blanket as I got dressed. The signal for the ceremony tonight would soon go off and I wanted to spend a few moments alone before I would be forced to put on a show for the town.

"We should head back."

"Veronica … I'm sorry," she muttered as she picked up the blanket, folding it up.

"It's okay," I whispered as I turned away from the lake to make my way back into town. But it wasn't okay. It was far from it.

Chapter 7

The world spun; music mixed with laughter. I wanted to laugh, to enjoy the night like all others in my town, but I could not. The man I danced with gripped my hand as he twirled me around, allowing me to see people staring at us. What did they see? Did we look happy? The twirls stopped and I faced Jax once more, his brown hair slightly tucked behind his ear as his brown eyes stared down at me.

There was a smile on his face as he led the dance. Was he enjoying dancing with me or was he envisioning my sister? My eyes flicked from Jax to Rory, who sat next to our parents. She poked at her food on her plate, not observing the dance floor. I bet it was hard on her. It was hard on me. I looked at Jax again as we moved our bodies to the music. He stared off into the distance. I didn't have to guess what he was staring at. I'd just stared at her myself. Jax didn't see me, he only saw my sister. But who could blame him? He was in love. I was just someone ruining it for everyone. Life was cruel.

I forced myself to look elsewhere, unable to keep staring at Jax, knowing he was looking at my sister. Instead, I focused on the surroundings, drinking in everyone's happiness, wishing it were mine.

People surrounding us on the dance floor, smiling as they swayed to the music with their partners, held no distance between their bodies as they let the music take control. On each corner of the dance floor was a wooden pillar, connected by wooden branches. Woven in between the branches were a variety of flowers. The dance floor would morph into where we would exchange our vows tomorrow. It would be a dream wedding that any woman would be blessed to have. Any woman but me. It felt like the beauty of it all was mocking.

"Are you okay?" Jax whispered.

I dragged my eyes from the flowers in the sky back to the man who still had his hands wrapped around my body. There was worry etched on his face, but I offered no response.

"Did you talk to Rory yet?"

I wanted to laugh; he didn't know the cat was out of the bag. Mother must have grabbed Rory away, preventing her chance of warning Jax.

The music paused as the musicians got ready to play another song. But the mood was ruined already. I pushed away from Jax's embrace and made my way off of the dance floor. Being on display was draining, and I just didn't have the mental capacity to deal with it.

"Veronica, over here!" a voice chimed, just barely escaping being muffled by the music starting up once more.

I turned to where Libby was waving like a madman, trying to get my attention. There was really only one person who could provide an escape, allowing me to be dragged from the thoughts that swarmed inside. A brief flash of a silver-haired man popped into my mind. So maybe there were two, but I didn't know where he was or if he even wanted to talk.

"Will you take a walk with me?" I asked immediately, reaching my hand out to her.

Leaving your own celebration and stealing my wife away? Should I be concerned?" Sam said. He was sitting next to Libby at the table, a big smile on his face as he helped his wife out of her seat.

"I don't know, Sam, maybe you should," I teased back. It was nice having the playful banter. It was different from everything else so far today.

"Just make sure she doesn't get hurt. As I'm sure you know, she is quite clumsy," Sam joked, as he finally helped Libby to her feet.

In return for his joke, he received a light smack on the shoulder, followed by a quick kiss on the cheek. It was always a delight to see the love shared between Libby and Sam. With her now free of the table, she clutched my hand as we made our way farther back, away from the crowd.

"Are you okay?" she whispered, doing her best to keep her voice down. The worry on her face grew with each step we took, for I still had not responded to her question. "Did Rory not find you? She promised she would talk to you," Libby pressed as I led her to the line of trees. It hid us from sight of everyone at the party, but we were close enough that the music still filled my ears. "What's going on?"

"Where would I even start?" I countered. There were a million things to say, but how did I go about doing so?

"Did you fix things between Rory and you?"

"I think the rift is beyond fixing," I said softly as I ran my free hand through my hair.

Libby tugged on my arm. "What happened? Talk to me. You're scaring me."

I hadn't wanted to tell her what was going on when she first came to my bedroom, but I really just needed someone to listen. I didn't know what to do. Jax was still in the dark about what was going on and had insisted it needed to be handled between sisters, but he could have told me.

Instead, he'd played along, going forward with the sham of a wedding knowing full well that my sister was in love with him.

If they had just come clean earlier, then maybe things could have changed. But waiting, not even wanting to tell me till I pushed, was what hurt the most. They were content to keep their secret, and that was what burned.

I helped Libby to the ground. My story would be long and I wanted her to be comfortable. Once she was leaning against the tree, I lay my head on her lap and she ran her fingers through my hair, calming my nerves. What had I done to be granted such a wonderful best friend? I would be forever grateful for her. Having her by my side was a blessing.

"Go ahead. I'm listening," she said softly, and that was the last straw.

The words spilled from my mouth, detailing the events of the past few days to her. I croaked out everything, all the memories playing in my head on repeat.

When there were no other words to utter, we sat in silence. She took it all in and offered a few words of wisdom, but I could tell she was just as shocked as I. It was a lot to process, and knowing that my wedding was tomorrow didn't give much time to figure out a way to set things straight. No, the path was already set, and there was nothing I could do but walk it.

The music died down. Soon a toast would be given to honor my sister. We had to be back beforehand or others would be worried. I grabbed Libby's hand and helped her to stand before we made our way out of the woods, back to Sam, still seated at the table. He stood and grabbed his wife's outstretched hand, helping her down into her seat.

I joined her at her side. I looked over to my parents to see them preparing for the toast, but Rory was not by them. I looked about, trying to find my little sister.

She was huddled in a corner, whispering to Jax. She must have been telling him that I knew, because his eyes were wide. My mother's toast filled the air and Jax started to walk away. He looked up, his eyes meeting mine, and I stared back. He made no move to join me at the table, and I dragged my attention to my mother as she continued to speak.

The secret had finally come to light, and now all parties involved knew.

CHAPTER 8

I leaned against the window, soaking in the sun's rays as I stared at the hustle and bustle below. The town was already gathered, ready for the exchange of vows, because it was finally the day of my wedding to Jax. I sighed as I maneuvered to stand in front of the mirror to admire my dress. With a twist to the left, I took in its beauty. It was a marvelous dress, but I no longer felt beautiful wearing it. It had been designed with my sister in mind to pay tribute to her, but now it just felt like poison against my skin.

"Can I come in?" a soft voice called through the door as Rory lightly knocked.

I turned to the closed door. Did I want to open it? I was still a ball of emotion, and that was never good. But it was Rory on the other side of the door. She was no longer hiding from me, and for that I could smile.

"Veronica?" she hesitantly asked as she knocked once more.

With a few quick steps, I covered the distance to the door and pulled it open. Her hazel eyes widened at seeing me in my wedding dress.

"You look really pretty," she mumbled.

I grabbed her hand and tugged her into my bedroom, closing the door behind her. I headed back to the open window to get some fresh air, once more leaning against it while I stared down at the crowd. I was due to make a grand entrance soon, but I didn't have butterflies in my stomach. I wasn't excited about this. I wasn't even sure I wanted this anymore. All of this was done so Rory could live her dream and explore the world.

"That is a beautiful hairpiece. Where did you get it?" she asked as I felt her fingers on my hair as she traced the flowers.

"A wedding gift from Libby," I answered as I turned to her.

The word *wedding* caused her to flinch and remove her hand.

A smile soon graced her face as she clasped her hands together. "That's nice."

She was good at hiding things. After all, it had taken me forever to figure out she was in love with Jax. Laughter filled the air outside as I kept my eyes trained on my younger sister, observing every movement she made.

"I am really glad for you. Jax is a good man," she said as she made her way over to my bed to sit, but her smile was forced.

Did she not think I would notice? We were both in pain.

Rory opened her mouth, quickly clamping it shut. She wanted to speak more, but she bit down on her lip. I sighed as I relaxed my position. We were walking on eggshells around each other. What a great way to spend our last day together. We would be forced to go our separate ways, unsure if we would ever cross paths again.

The longer I stared at Rory, the more it dawned on me: the whole reason I'd decided to get married in the first place was so she could be offered and get the chance to explore the world. I had done all of this for her, my precious little sister. I didn't want the day to go on like this, for this to be our last memory together, unable to even speak to each other. It would be something I would forever regret.

I made my way over to the bed, sitting right next to Rory, who attempted to put distance between us, but I grabbed her hands, preventing her from doing so.

"Do you truly love him?" I asked.

"I'm so sorry! I never meant for any of this to happen, I swear!" she blurted as tears fell from her eyes.

I brought my hand up to wipe some of the tears from her cheek. She was in so much pain and I hated that I was so preoccupied with my own pain to not truly see she was suffering alongside me.

"I don't want you to hate me," she muttered.

"I could never."

"I want things to go back to normal."

"They will."

"But we have no time…" she sobbed as she threw herself into my chest, wrapping her arms around my waist. She did nothing to contain her sobs. But she was right—time had run out. A wedding still had to take place, and an offering still had to be made to the vampires. I continued holding her, swaying slightly, as she emptied her pent-up emotions. If only we had done this days ago.

It was quite a bit of time before her sobs stopped and she was able to compose herself, removing herself from my chest as she wiped at her eyes.

"I should get going so you can finish getting ready," she said as she got up.

But I wasn't ready to be alone again. I tugged her back, so she was once more sitting on the bed.

"Do you truly love Jax?" I asked once more.

"It's just a schoolgirl's crush. I'll get over it." She had a broken smile on her face.

"Don't lie to me. Aren't you tired of keeping secrets from me?" I bit out, but I pressed on. "Do you truly love Jax?"

"Yes…" she answered.

"And Jax truly loves you?"

"Yes…"

"And will you live happily ever after if you were to marry?" I asked.

"We can't marry," she answered, but I squeezed her hands, urging her to answer my question, so I asked once more.

"Would you and Jax live happily ever after if you were to marry?"

"I hope so."

I sighed as I let go of her hands, opting to run my fingers through my hair, doing my best to not ruin the style. But it didn't really matter anymore, because I wasn't going to be getting married. I stood and immediately got to work removing the dress.

"What are you doing?" Rory questioned.

"Get undressed."

The dress fell to the floor and I yanked the comb gifted from Libby from my hair and threw it on the bed. Rory was still confused; she made no movement. But we didn't have time. Drastic measures were all we had left. I wrapped my fingers around the hem of Rory's shirt, yanking it above her head before quickly throwing it over my shoulder.

"Don't make me do the pants as well," I said as I crossed my arms.

She stood in a daze as she removed her pants, letting them fall to the ground, not needing any other prompting. I picked them up and threw them on, before heading over to my wardrobe. I needed a coat, for if I was to step outside in the clothes of those who are offered, it would spark confusion, which would lead to questions, which always led to time being wasted, and time was a rare currency.

My fingers brushed the soft black material of one of my hooded coats. With it quickly thrown on, I turned to face Rory to see how the dress would look on her. But she still hadn't put the dress on, opting to just stand there gobsmacked. A slew of curses flew from under my breath as I made my way over to her and forced her into the dress.

"What are you doing?"

I paid her no mind. I grabbed the jewelry piece from the bed and, with a few twists of her hair, had the flower piece on full display.

"Stop! We can't!" She whirled around, grabbing my hands.

"You love Jax, so marry him," I said as a smile spread across my face.

"We can't!" she shot back.

"Why not?"

"I'm the offering. Someone has to be offered."

"Why do you think I'm wearing these clothes in the first place?" I said, letting a laugh escape. It was nice to finally be able to spend time with Rory, just as it was before everything fell apart. I didn't want our last day to end in regrets, and I was glad it wasn't going to.

Realization dawned on her as she made her way to stand in front of my mirror, taking a moment to see herself in a wedding dress. The garment was never meant for me; it was truly made for her to wear. It was as if the world had sent me hints to get the dress made in her favorite color because she was always the one meant to walk down the aisle.

"How do I look?" she asked hesitantly as she twirled, trying to see every angle of herself.

"Absolutely breathtaking," I answered, the smile on her face absolutely worth it. "Go be happy, little sister."

"Thank you…"

I wrapped my arms around her to give her one last hug. I wouldn't be able to linger and watch her get married. I needed to get out of town as soon as possible before everyone realized what was going on.

I made my way back to my wardrobe for a bag to bring some items. I wasn't sure exactly what I would need, but I stuffed some random items in there, as well as my dagger from Libby.

With one last smile in Rory's direction, I headed to the door, grasped the doorknob in my hand, and yanked it open. It was time to start my next adventure.

CHAPTER 9

L eaving my home would be the simple part. The hard part was about to start. It had sounded easy when I was in the room with Rory—simply trading spots would solve all of our problems. But I still needed to get out of town as soon as possible or everything would be nothing and we would be forced to walk our miserable paths. At least with a decision, a fresh path was carved for me, one where I didn't know what lay ahead and all I could do was put one foot in front of the other. But at least for my dear little sister and Jax, their path would be one of happiness.

Standing on the front steps, I scanned the area, waiting for people to leave the road I needed to take so I could start putting some distance between my home and me. When someone dropped something on the ground and people rushed to help, I took that as my opportunity. Doing my best to keep my head down—but not too far down as that would cause people to get suspicious—I clutched my bag tightly to my side, trying to morph it into my body so it didn't *look* like I was skipping town, and started my trek.

People started to thin out the farther I got from the center of the town. Everyone was making their way to where the wedding would be held, which left the outer banks of town easier to maneuver in. It would be the last time I traveled the paths that I had every day since I could walk. There would be no more playing with Rory in the fields, or running to Libby's house so we could hang out. No more antics from Mother for having a daughter who wasn't the image of a lady and the opposite from Father, who didn't care how we grew up, only that we were healthy. Tears brimmed at the edge of my eyes as my family, Libby included, would no longer be a constant in my life. But what hurt the most was having to leave without saying goodbye. Would they understand my choice? Would they be mad?

Dragged from my thoughts as the gate came into view, I picked up my pace. I needed to leave before anyone caught me, but most importantly: before I got cold feet and turned back. My coat billowed out and my hood threatened to fall back, but I held on as I pushed past the gate to my new life—one where the only thing on my path forward was a horse and a bunch of trees. It wasn't a promising new start, but I was only a few steps outside of town. I stared at the horse as I made my way over to the animal. Could I just get on the horse and ride off into the distance, not looking back?

I threw my bag on the horse, tying it down so it wouldn't get loose from the long journey ahead. I doubted I would be able to just ride off into the unknown. Unless I wanted to ruin Rory's wedding, someone had to be an offering. With a sigh, putting my foot in the stirrup, I hoisted myself up. Or at least attempted to, for the horse sidestepped to avoid my attempt at mounting. I'd probably confused it. The horse didn't know me. But we needed to become fast friends because I could not be sitting outside the gates or it would all too easy for everyone to find me. So I tried again, stuffing my foot into the stirrup as I pulled myself up. Immediately the horse kicked out, my foot swung from the sudden movement, and then I was on my back, staring at the sky.

I closed my eyes, trying to calm my rapidly beating heart. It was just nerves. The horse could probably read the nervous vibes radiating from me and wanted nothing to do with me. I felt a shift next to me; the sun no longer blasted against my eyelids. I cracked one eye open, before opening both to stare into a pool of silver. A person stood over me, blocking the sun, his equally silver hair blowing in the wind. Watching me was starting to feel like it was a habit of his. He'd done the same at the river, watching from the bank.

"Hi," I muttered as I stood. It was our third time meeting, and I still didn't know his name.

"What are you doing?" he asked as he took a few steps forward to run his hand along the horse.

"I kind of need to put some distance between me and the town. I was going to take the horse for a quick ride," I blurted out as I went to unbuckle my bag. But his hand reached out, stopping my movement.

"Running away?"

"Not exactly. I'm the offering."

"No, you aren't," he said as he maneuvered himself to stand in front of me, staring down.

I was the new offering and no one would have any say in it. This was my decision, and my other way to ensure that Rory got her happily ever after.

"I'm the *new* offering." I said, hoping he would just get the hint and not ask any questions.

He stood still, observing me, causing my nerves to act up. Did they have some sort of requirement to be an offering? I hadn't heard anything about it, but then again I wasn't the one who'd read up all about vampires. That was Rory. With the haste of our swap, I didn't think to ask for a crash course on what to expect. I was dragged from my thoughts as I heard voices from the town. Panic surged inside and I bit down on my lip. The ruse was up. If they caught me outside the gate, that would be the end of it.

"Please. Can we go?" Urgency laced every word I spoke.

I didn't want to be dragged back to go through a sham wedding to a man who couldn't love me. Before I could beg once more, the man mounted the horse with ease and reached out his hand to help me up. This time, the horse didn't move and let me up easily.

"Now you let me up," I muttered under my breath, as I wrapped my arms around the man whose name I still didn't know.

"Of course not. I trained him better than that," he said as he urged the horse forward, starting us on a slow trot.

"Could we go a bit faster? I'm in a bit of a hurry."

"In a hurry to be an offering?"

"We could go with that."

He didn't question further; he dug his heels in, and our speed increased. The wind blew in my face as I leaned into the man, trying to block some of it, my arms tightening around his waist to prevent being thrown off the back of the horse. The trees passed in a blur, and if I dared to look back over my shoulder, the gate would be getting smaller. I was finally riding off into the next chapter of my life.

But all that came to a halt when our pace slowed to the point we were about to come to a complete stop.

"Why have we stopped?"

"I need to wait for the rest of my men."

"How long till they arrive?" I asked as he slid off the horse. I followed suit. We weren't going to be moving for a bit. "Don't you need to tie up your horse?" I asked as he walked over to a tree and sat down, closing his eyes.

I stared at him, unsure of what I was supposed to be doing. We were two people unfamiliar with each other in an unfamiliar place. While we were still close to town, there would be no way for me to make any sense of where to go, for I had never ventured alone into the woods before. Accepting my fate that I had nothing else to do but wait, I made my way over to the tree the man sat under.

"Where exactly are we going?"

"You ask a lot of questions."

"Is asking a lot of questions bad?" I responded to his remark as I sat on the ground. The shade provided some cool from the sun. With no idea of where we were heading or how long it would take for us to get there, I might as well enjoy the break. The man beside me kept his eyes closed, acting like he had not heard my questions, but I needed some answers.

"What does it mean to be an offering?" Moments passed in silence. "Hello?" This time, I raised my voice, irritation evident from being ignored.

He cracked an eye open and looked at me.

I had finally gotten his attention. "What's going to happen to me? If you haven't noticed, I don't really know what's going on." I crossed my arms, my eyes never leaving his one opened eye.

"I don't know."

"What do you mean you don't know? How can you not know?"

"I'm a retriever. I don't care what happens to the offering after my part is done. Hence I don't know." He closed his eye once more, leaving me alone to sit in silence.

Chapter 10

The gray castle was the biggest building I had ever laid eyes on. It was also one of the most intimidating, for not only was it huge, it was spooky. Darkness seemed drawn to it, adding to the creepiness factor as we rode closer. It reached well into the sky, causing me to crane my head back quite far to see all of it. Vines covered a decent portion of it, but instead of adding a layer of life with the green vines usually were, these were brown. Either they didn't do maintenance on their home often, or they preferred it that way. It truly was an enchanting look, one of darkness with a hint of an earthy tone.

The silver-haired man with the equally silver eyes pushed forward, urging the horse we shared to go straight through the castle gates. From what I could see, the walls would circle the castle, but just how big was this place?

"So glad to be back!" one of the men in the group exclaimed.

I turned to look at him. We'd had to wait for the rest of the group to return before we could start on our journey, and in the group were a total of two other vampires. Or at least I assumed they were vampires. They weren't the men I'd seen the silver-haired man in company of at the tavern, and I hadn't seen them in town.

The man I shared a horse with dismounted before making his way up the castle steps. A loud creaking noise filled the air as I whirled my head around to look at the castle gates slowly starting to close on their own.

An unsettling feeling grew in the pit of my stomach. What had I gotten myself into? The silver-haired man stopped right before the castle doors. As he turned to look at me, I slid off the horse. Everything around me was unfamiliar, and if gates could close on their own, I didn't want to be left alone to figure out what else could move. Right now, the silver-haired man was the only thing familiar and the only one who dared speak to me, even if it was just a few words during the trip here.

I rushed right up the stairs, not caring what the others of our party were going to do. And if he didn't tie up his horse back in the woods, there was no need to do so in a castle. There was nowhere it could go anyway, if the gate was closed.

"Thought you were going to take all night," he muttered as he turned and opened the doors wide open.

At least the doors of the castle didn't open on their own.

"What's going on?" I asked as I followed him into the castle.

My nerves were growing with each step forward. Did Rory know about this and she'd still wanted to be an offering? I scrunched up my face—it was even darker inside the castle.

"Good luck." The silver-haired man smirked as he grabbed my bag and disappeared into the darkness. One second he was there and the next he wasn't, and now I was truly alone in an unfamiliar place that set my nerves on edge.

"There you are! This way! We are late!" a voice chimed in the opposite direction from which the man had disappeared.

I whirled around, trying to find the source of the voice so I wouldn't have to be in the dark alone. A girl stood in a hallway that was strangely lit, not to the point I could see everything but enough that I could see several steps in front of me. But it wasn't like that moments ago...

"Let's go!" she exclaimed as she grabbed my hand, yanking me down the hallway. "I'm glad I got here in time! It would have been bad if you'd walked off on your own. You should be more careful."

I wasn't going to be alone. I had every intention of not exploring the dark castle on my own. I would have run after the silver-haired man, but I had a feeling if I attempted to follow him, I would be in an even worse situation.

"I'm so happy you're here!"

I focused on the girl dragging me down an unfamiliar hallway that had been just a dark void before her arrival. Her red hair was a contrast to the dark we were surrounded by, her green eyes twinkling every time she looked over her shoulder to speak to me. The most peculiar thing, though, was what she was wearing. She wore a simple, somewhat loose fitting, burgundy dress that left very little of her legs covered; even the back was exposed.

"Why are you dressed like that?" I asked, truly wondering why she was wearing so few clothes. She didn't even have shoes!

"Like what?" she asked, as she stopped to examine herself.

Obviously, she didn't find anything wrong with her dress, so I guess I shouldn't be one to judge. I was just curious, for it was an odd piece of very revealing clothing to be worn out in the open.

"Don't worry, you will get a dress as well!"

"Uh…" I muttered back. That wasn't why I was asking about her dress though.

"I've got to get you ready! We're already behind schedule."

"Ready for what exactly?"

"I'm so excited to have another girl to talk to! It gets a bit lonely sometimes!"

"Are there no other girls here?" I hesitantly asked, unsure if I really wanted an answer.

"There are others. I tend to keep company others like to steer clear of," she whispered, shooting a smile in my direction.

She didn't elaborate on just want company she kept that caused others to stay away, but just from my brief time spent with her, she seemed like a good friend to have. My first friend in this new place I would be living…

I stared at her as we finally slowed our pace. "What's your name, by the way?"

"It's Nadine, and you are Veronica!"

"Wait, how do you know my name? We swapped offerings last minute."

"Right, that hasn't happened before, at least of what I am aware of. But we did receive word about the change from the retriever."

The silver-haired man had sent word prior to our arrival? We were glued to each other's sides since we met up in the woods. I would have noticed if he had sent a message ahead. Or did he know there was a possibility of a switch and that was why he didn't question it too much when we left town? So many questions ran through my head as I tried to piece together what exactly was going to happen in this castle. But all of that came to a screeching halt when Nadine opened the door we had arrived at.

Eyes wide, I took in the room. On the wall opposite us as soon as we entered was a huge stained glass mural that converted the moonlight from outside into a display of wonderful colors. But that wasn't all that was in the room, for in the center was a bunch of pillows on the ground and a bunch of girls sat on them who were dressed exactly like Nadine. My face scrunched as I scanned the room. This was the normal attire of everyone here? A few tables lined the wall to the left, and as I took a few more steps into the room, I could see it contained an array of refreshments and food. On the right, though, as I craned my head to look in that direction, were several doors.

"What is this place?"

"It's called the gathering room because it's where we gather!" Nadine said, following up with a laugh.

The meaning of the room could easily be gleaned from the name of the room, but I would let Nadine have her moment. Once more, she grabbed my hand, then led me in the direction of the closed doors on the right side of the room.

"Everyone else is already ready, so you have the bathroom to yourself! Just don't take too long!" she exclaimed as she opened the door, and pushed me inside, promptly closing the door behind me.

My mouth dropped at the sight of the biggest bathroom I'd ever seen in my life. A grand bathroom meant for sharing, as there were several spots to shower. Each provided privacy, so at least it wasn't a communal shower. A quick shower to brush away the grime, and a bit of finger de-tangling had me looking refreshed and not like I'd just had several days' journey to get here.

On the counter was a towel, and underneath it was gold cloth. Wrapping the towel around my body in case someone did enter the bathroom, I picked up the gold garment. Nadine had said I would have my own dress soon enough, and it was true, for in my hands was the same exact dress she wore, but not in red. Just like hers, it didn't cover much, leaving little to the imagination.

I scanned the room, trying to find something else to wear, but the only choices were the dirty clothes I'd arrived in, a towel, or the gold dress. I let loose a deep sigh as I slid into the dress, followed by the undergarments they'd provided.

"Are you almost done in there?" Nadine's voice filtered through the closed bathroom door as I stood staring at myself in the mirror. Technically, I was done, but I didn't want to be. I wanted something more to cover up with. While gold was a good color on me, it was also a bright color that would make me stand out. Which might not be the best thing in this new unsettling surrounding. The door creaked open as Nadine's mop of red hair poked in.

"Let's go! We don't want to keep the Grand Elder waiting much longer!" she chimed as she poked back out, leaving me to hurry behind her.

"Who is the Grand Elder and where are we going dressed like this?" I asked as I entered the gathering room, which was now empty save for Nadine and myself. The other girls had already left. We were truly late.

"All the offerings are to be presented," Nadine answered as she grabbed my hand, dragging me from the gathering room and out into the hallway.

"Presented to the Grand Elder, I presume?"

"Yes, you got it!"

"Who is the Grand Elder?" I asked as we made progress down the hallway to wherever our destination was.

"The leader, of course."

I nodded along. Of course it made sense we would need to meet the person in charge. We didn't call our leader Grand Elder, so why would I know that is what they did here? I was really starting to wish I'd known more about vampires before hastily switching places with Rory.

It was too late to turn back time. Nadine, wasting no time, shoved me through the doors into the darkness.

Chapter 11

My heart raced as I tried to wipe some of the sweat off my hands onto my dress. The amount of uncomfortableness I was feeling was through the roof as Nadine dragged me into the room to stand in line with the other girls—a single file line of all the girls in a dark room where we couldn't even see how big the room actually was. Why was everything so dark in this castle? The only source of light was from a single window straight ahead that was doing a magical job of highlighting the females but nothing else. The definition of spooky was this castle.

Thankfully, Nadine stood to my right, allowing me to not be at the end of the line. One never wanted to be first or last, especially when everything else around was darkness.

"This is a bit uncomfortable. What is going on?" I hissed.

The *bit* was an understatement, but I wasn't sure if there were other people in the room with us. As if sensing my thoughts, there was a movement under the window and a figure appeared. I peered over the shoulder of the man, but all around was darkness. Was there a door under the window? If so, we should have seen some indication of it being opened, which could only mean he'd been here the whole time. My heart throbbed as I clutched my chest, trying to get a grip.

I looked at the man who had appeared. He stood under the window scanning the line of girls. He was a man of similar height to me, but so very skinny that it made him look sick. His jet-black hair was slicked back, a contrast to his pale skin, but almost matching the deep bags under his eyes.

"Don't worry, this will be quick!" Nadine whispered next to me, but I kept my eyes trained on the man before us.

She was starting to seem like a ball of sunshine that was never fazed. Before, she'd mentioned that people didn't like the company she kept, but I was starting to think it was she who scared people away. For if she was a ball of happiness in a castle like this one, there had to be something wrong with her.

My stomach dropped, an uneasy feeling coming over me as the man stared back at me, his beady black eyes setting off every internal alarm possible. I wanted to leave, but my body was rooted, unwilling to budge. He stared for a moment longer, before smiling, exposing his gray teeth as he shifted his gaze to Nadine and finally off me. Feeling rushed back to my body, no longer the center of attention, but I knew I didn't want to cross paths with the Grand Elder often.

"Welcome, girls! We are pleased to have you here!" he bellowed, throwing his arms out in greeting. Glowing red eyes appeared in the darkness from all corners of the room as the Grand Elder came closer to the line. I held my breath as the realization dawned on me. We had never been alone in this room. He started at the left, slowly making his way down the line, only stopping briefly at me before reaching his hand to Nadine.

"Grand Elder," she said as she grabbed his hand. *This was the company she kept?* "I have prepared the girls as asked."

The pain in my chest was still present but now I felt sick, watching the Grand Elder give Nadine a smile. The man looked intimidating under the moonlight, but standing so close to him made him look like he had come back to life from the dead. His skin was not just pale but contained a gray tone.

"Yes, Nadine, thank you very much," he said as he brought Nadine's hand to his mouth and placed a kiss that lingered for several uncomfortable moments, which caused her to smile and bring her other hand up to her cheek.

I really was going to be sick. There would be no way I could stand him, let alone hold his hand like Nadine was currently doing. He let go of her hand and she stepped back in line while he went back to stand under the window.

"An interesting crop we have this month," he started, his eyes pausing on every girl as he made his way down the line. "We even have a volunteer, someone who swapped last minute," he said, as his eyes landed on me once more, sending shocks up my spine. The silver-haired man, or even the others in the travel party, had never set off alarm bells in me like the Grand Elder did.

"A few of you are not fit for this society, so you will be sent back home."

A few of the girls in line attempted to whisper to one another, doing a horrible job of keeping their voices low. They were overjoyed that there was a chance they could go home, but I knew better. I didn't know much about vampires, but I did know once someone was offered, they never came back. Promises uttered by the Grand Elder would be taken with a grain of salt.

"Every morning, you will be required to donate a bit of blood. We have to make sure we didn't get damaged goods," the man said, sending the girls again into a flurry of whispers.

I kept my mouth shut. I had already drawn enough attention by being a last-minute swap. The less I was on this man's radar, the better, but the gears in my head started to spin. Why did we have to donate every day? Surely that wasn't healthy for someone, and the mention of damaged goods did little to settle my nerves.

"Damaged goods?" a girl blurted out, but I didn't dare try to see who had spoken.

"Yes. Vampires can be quite picky with their blood," the Grand Elder responded as his eyes narrowed.

"Vampires?" The same girl from before spoke up, but this time I really wanted to know who was speaking.

"Do you live under a rock?" the Grand Elder spat out, and I was wondering the same thing.

I didn't know much about vampires, but the girl who'd spoken sounded like she had no idea of what was really going on, and if that was case, she was in a worse position than I.

"You will be required to spend time with the residents here in hopes of finding a match."

From the corner of my vision, I could see someone slowly raise their hand, as if this were a classroom and they were trying to get the teacher's attention. Due to his earlier annoyance and comment, she must have been put off from blurting out again, for she didn't speak but kept her hand raised.

"Finding a match is very important. You will only have one month," the man continued, ignoring the girl with her hand raised.

I felt bad for her. I knew the feeling of having unanswered questions and just wanting things to make sense.

"Nadine, take them back to the gathering room," he said, and the red eyes that had once filled the dark space disappeared, leaving just us girls and the Grand Elder.

Wasting no time at all, Nadine turned to the door and marched off. Not wanting to stay in the same room as the man who could send shivers through my body, I ran after her, the other girls close on our heels. The sound of a creaking door drew my attention, causing me to look over my shoulder, but I wished I hadn't for the Grand Elder was still standing there, illuminated by the light shining through the sole window of the room, a grin on his face. But that wasn't the most alarming sight, for his beady black eyes were now a vibrant red. I whirled my head back around and increased my speed. I didn't know what that room was, but I didn't want to step foot in there again. We made it back to the gathering room in record time, a few girls opting to collapse on the pillows on the ground while I grabbed Nadine's hand to get her attention and let loose a slew of questions.

"Damaged goods? Daily blood? One month for a match? Can you explain what the heck is going on here?"

Chapter 12

S leep had evaded me till the very last minute. I rolled to my
side, staring at the blank wall that had a small window to
allow some light in my room. Each of us got our own room to
allow some sense of privacy, but it was the size of a shoebox. It
only allowed a bed, desk with a chair, and a chest.

I sighed, bringing my hands up to cover my face, blocking the
light. After the meeting with the Grand Elder, Nadine hadn't
answered any of my questions, which had left me all night trying
to process what was going to happen within the castle walls.
Some of us would be sent home supposedly, and the ones who
stayed had to donate blood every day to find a match—according
to the Grand Elder, a man who sent shivers coursing through my
body just thinking about him.

I moved my hands away from my face to look at my door as it
creaked open. A very familiar redheaded girl with green eyes
poked her head through the crack, shooting a smile in my
direction. She wore the same burgundy dress from yesterday, but
it wasn't exactly the same. Upon arriving at my room last night,
I'd searched every nook and cranny, which didn't take long.
When searching the chest, though, I had found several pieces of

the same gold dress I wore. It seemed the dresses weren't just arrival clothing, but to be worn at all time.

"You *are* awake! Why didn't you join us in the gathering room?" Nadine said as she fully let herself into my room.

I stared at her. I knew I was late, but I didn't have the will to go to the gathering room again. She walked over to the end of my bed, a proud smile on her face. After the events of yesterday, I was sure Nadine wasn't fazed by the expectations of us being offered. After all, she kept company with the Grand Elder. She grabbed my hand, forcing me from my bed.

"We need to get our blood drawn for the day before we can do anything else." She sounded more chipper than last night as she pulled me from my bedroom.

I was barely able to close the door behind me in her rush. There weren't any valuables in my room due to the silver-haired man taking my bag upon arrival. The man who'd disappeared into the darkness before my very eyes. Was he also in that room last night?

Nadine led the way to the nurse. "I know it was a lot to take in yesterday, but you'll get the hang of it!"

I wasn't sure I wanted to get the hang of it, because that meant I would be staying. I was so lost in my thoughts that I didn't notice we'd arrived at the double doors of an office. Nadine greeted a lady sitting behind a desk. The lady wrote away at her desk while Nadine let go of my hand and made her way over to sit on an exam table.

The woman behind the desk had hair just like the Grand Elder —slicked-back, jet-black hair. She finished her task and raised her face to look in our direction. I studied her as she pushed out of her chair to go to the table where Nadine waited. Unlike the Grand Elder and more like the silver-haired man, her skin had color, still slightly pale, but she didn't look like death. She must have taken better care of her health, for there were no dark circles under her eyes, and when she smiled at Nadine, her teeth were white. Knowing that the person I had to see every day wasn't as creepy looking as the Grand Elder calmed my nerves slightly as I walked closer to the exam table.

"Morning, ladies. You are the last two for the day and then I'm off." She maneuvered a tray with medical supplies closer to Nadine. "You must be Veronica," she said, without taking her eyes off Nadine, picking up a needle. One vial later and it was my turn. She motioned to the exam table as she got to work prepping another needle. "I'm Amelia. It's nice to meet you, Veronica. We have taken a bit of blood today since today is your first day. If you feel faint, don't worry, the other days will only be a vial or two."

The nurse, Amelia, wrapped her fingers around my arm and stuck the first needle in.

It was a small shot of pain, but it quickly went away. If I looked at the needle, the pain would come back, so I focused my attention on looking around the office. It was a small room, and every corner was visible—no impenetrable darkness, thankfully. Three exam tables lined the left wall of the office, each with a separation curtain all the way pushed back. On the opposite side were her desk and a few chairs.

Along the back wall, medicine cabinets bordered both sides of the window. Like the gathering room, it was a stained-glass window that tinted the light that shone through. Under the window was a table with two chairs. The castle had a theme going on. Room would either be cast in darkness or lit by glowing tinted windows.

"I heard you were a last-minute offering. What changed?" Amelia asked as I heard her move things around on the tray before pressure was applied once more to my skin.

"My sister fell in love, so I took her spot," I said quietly, keeping my eyes straight ahead.

"That is nice of you. Who was getting married?"

"I was." This time, my voice was even quieter.

I hadn't had time to think about Rory and Jax since my arrival, too busy trying to consume information about my new life. The pressure on my arm lightened, and I turned to the nurse to see if she was done.

Her eyes met mine as she took a step back. "So you gave up your happily-ever-after so your sister could have hers? I would say that's a first here." Amelia pushed the tray with our vials of blood to the back wall where the cabinets were.

"Well, when your sister falls in love with your soon-to-be husband, there isn't much you can do."

Amelia whipped her head around to look in my direction while Nadine gasped at my side. I guess people knew I was a last-minute offering, but not the reason why I was one.

"Did you love him?" Amelia asked, concern etched on her face.

"No."

"I never knew!" Nadine exclaimed as she latched on to my arm.

"Seems things worked out in the end. Do you feel like you are going to faint?" Amelia asked.

I shook my head, no. It didn't feel like I would pass out, but I could feel the pressure at the edges of my mind. If Amelia had taken more blood, I might have fainted.

"That's good. You have a good tolerance level, which will come in handy."

"Why is that good?" I questioned. I was to have my blood drawn every day, but only a vial or two from what she'd previously said. Why would she say having a tolerance was a good thing? But most importantly, when did it come into play?

Her voice was calm as she spoke: "Because your chances of survival just increased."

She didn't look at me, opting to continue messing with the medicine cabinet. I looked over to Nadine to see if she was also hearing the same thing I was. As soon as our eyes made contact, she looked away, pretending to look at something else.

"Am I at risk here?" I pressed on. I needed answers.

My arrival was a last-minute decision, which left me lacking knowledge of what exactly I was walking into. Amelia stopped messing with the cabinet, turning to face me, a smile on her face.

"Of course. You're in the den of vampires, after all. It's best you girls hurry along."

Nadine needed no further prompting, latching on to me once more and dragging me from the nurse's office, Amelia watching us as we left.

At home, we all assumed being offered was a good thing. We were told stories that once someone was offered, they got the chance to travel the world, and lived a life of luxury. But my brief time here told me that was a lie. Combined with Amelia's statement, I knew I was in trouble.

Chapter 13

I lay on the cushion watching Nadine as she made a plate of food. Immediately upon returning to the gathering room, I'd brought Nadine over to a set of cushions, fully intent on questioning her. Questions were building up and there weren't enough answers being shared. But the rumbling of stomachs caused a slight delay. There would be no harm in waiting a minute or two till we had some food in our stomachs.

"I got a bit of everything," Nadine said as she sat down beside me.

Picking myself back up, I grabbed a handful of fruit and popped a few berries in my mouth.

"Can you tell me more about this place?" I asked, keeping my voice low.

The other girls were in the room with us. I hadn't had the pleasure of meeting them, and because of that I didn't want to be caught talking about this place out loud.

"Depends on what you want to know," Nadine answered as she grabbed a pastry and bit into it.

I watched her, my face scrunching up. Sometimes people would give answers, vague ones, but answers nonetheless. Other times, the questions would be deflected. But all that did was increase my curiosity about what was happening in the castle. With hopes of getting information out of Nadine before she deflected, I started off easy.

"Why so much blood the first time?"

"It's for the matching."

"And why exactly are we being matched?" I questioned as I thought back to the conversation with the Grand Elder.

He'd mentioned we had to spend time with the residents in order to find a match. Yet he didn't provide other information on why it was important to do so, only that we had one month. If we didn't find a match, what happened after the one month?

"Everyone gets their blood drawn in order for the vampires to sample it. That is how they determine if you are a match or not." She nodded as if this was common knowledge.

It wasn't.

"So they're testing to see which vampires like my blood? Why is that important?"

"Because if you get matched, you become their personal blood bank!" She beamed a smile in my direction.

Becoming someone's personal blood bank wasn't exactly on my to-do list. And if it was, it would be the very last item.

"So they like my blood and that makes us matched? That's it?"

"No, not really. Some vampires like to develop relationships with their blood banks," she said, her cheeks reddening as she shifted.

Instantly, I knew what she was talking about, but the only vampire I'd seen Nadine interact with was the Grand Elder. And that was not a pretty picture in my head.

"If the vampire can't stand to be around you, then they won't match with you."

I nodded. That was probably my best option. Get all the vampires to not like me so I wouldn't be forced to match and become someone's personal blood supply. If that was the outcome I wanted, then I needed to find out what happened when one didn't match.

"If we don't find a match, what happens?" I asked.

Nadine stopped eating and brought her hand to cup her chin.

"Well, it depends," she answered, starting on her food once more.

Again with the deflected answers. *Well, it depends* could either have meant a million things or just a handful of things.

My eyes rolled her antics. "And what exactly does it depend on?"

"Depends if a vampire likes you or not. If one likes you, then you get to hang out around here. If not, you're gone."

I perked up. "So even if my matched doesn't like me, if a single vampire has taken a liking to me, then I stay? And *gone*? Gone where?" I needed to revise my plan. Having every single vampire dislike me in the castle would be a tall order, especially since I had already met Amelia.

If I had to see her every day, it would be hard to be annoying all the time, especially since she was nice.

"I don't know."

"To which part? The staying or going?"

"I don't know where someone goes once they aren't picked."

"Nadine, you really have *no* idea?" I questioned.

It was hard to believe that someone who hung out with the Grand Elder didn't know what happened to the girls when they weren't picked.

"Nope!" she chirped out, and started on her food once more.

A sigh escaped as I watched her. I doubted she would provide more details about the matching process. A change in topic was needed.

"Is there anything to look forward to around here? Other than being a blood bank?" I quickly added in the last piece as her face brightened at my question.

I already knew she liked the benefits of being a personal blood supply, but I had no intention of being one.

"Spending time with the vampires is the main thing. They take you on dates and treat you like a princess. I have one I like, a real Prince Charming. Not an actual prince, but we do have one of those here," she said as she brought her hand up to her flushed cheek.

I stared at the redheaded girl. She either had a few screws loose or was completely smitten with her vampire. An image of the Grand Elder with his slicked-back black hair allowing one to perfectly see his beady black eyes and equally dark eye bags popped up in my mind. Him next to Nadine. Who had vibrant red hair, green eyes, and flushed skin.

I didn't want to pry. You love who you love, but I definitely had questions. Questions I wasn't sure if it would be better to have answers or not, for the image was already hard enough to deal with.

"Are we allowed to explore?" I asked.

I needed the image of the Grand Elder out of my mind, and the best way was to change the topic.

"Not really! But I know a few places we can sneak away to." Nadine grabbed my hand, pulling us both up, before leaving the gathering room.

The night of my arrival, the castle was a foreboding building and still was,—darkness in every corner and magical moving gates. Thankfully, in the daytime, light shone into the castle hallways. But there was still darkness. The vampires liked it dark.

Our feet padded against the floor as we made our way to our destination. Even though it had been hard to see when I met the Grand Elder in that room, I knew we were making our way in that direction.

It was still vivid in my mind, that meeting: the way he appeared in the dark, the red eyes that lurked in the corner, us girls in a line on display … a shiver rocked up my spine, the Grand Elder coming to the forefront of my mind. He might be old, older than Amelia and the silver-haired man, but he was dangerous. Way more dangerous than the other two. And I would do my best to steer clear of him.

The door to the room we stood in last night was cracked open slightly, allowing me a brief look in as we walked past. Just like last night, the room was etched in darkness, despite it being daylight. The only source of light came from the small window.

I tugged on Nadine's hand, drawing her to a halt as I walked back to the room. Bringing my face closer to the crack, I peered inside. Was this another magical ability of the castle or was there truly not another source of light in there? Rows of red eyes had stared at us, so it was big in there, but the question was how big? But more importantly, what exactly was the room used for? It was impossible to have a look around, something I wouldn't have done in the Grand Elder's presence, but he wasn't here right now. If he was, I would feel the tingles in my spine, for his mere presence scared me.

I pushed the door slightly, which allowed for a better view of the pitch dark room. I took a step inside as I tossed a look over my shoulder, needing to confirm that Nadine was still by my side. She let out a gasp. I whirled back around and my face smacked right into a chest of someone who was taller than me. Hands gripped my waist, preventing me from stumbling back. I dragged my eyes up the black, skintight shirt the man wore, straight to the smirk and the green pools staring down at me.

I gulped. He smiled, his teeth on display. He was definitely a vampire. It was official: I had met four vampires. The fact I was living among vampires was being hammered into my head. There was no escaping them.

"What are you doing here?" the man said, his voice deep, shaking me to my core.

I stared back at him, unable to form words. Even if I could, what would I say: *Curiosity got the best of me, so I helped myself to entering this room*? Yeah, I doubted that would go over well.

"Can't talk?" the man asked, stepping closer. His hot breath bore down at me, but the longer I stared the more I was reminded of the Grand Elder. He wasn't as pale, or have the deep, dark bags, but what they did have in common was their presence. The man before me wasn't as overbearing as the leader of the vampires, but give it a few years, or maybe it was centuries, and he would invoke the same response in me as the Grand Elder.

"Donovan! I'm so glad to see you!" Nadine shouted as she raced past me to latch on to the man before me.

My eyes were wide as I stared at the redhaired girl. Now I understood perfectly why everyone stayed clear of her, for she truly did keep bad company. First it was the Grand Elder and now this Donovan person? Both of them oozed bad energy.

Donovan leaned down to place a kiss right on Nadine's lips. Their moment was passionate, for he deepened his kiss, wrapping his hand around Nadine's waist, bringing her in close.

Instinctively, I took a step back. One wrong move and I would wind up ruining their moment. Was this the person who had made Nadine blush from her thoughts earlier, back in the gathering room? If so, Donovan was definitely several steps better than the Grand Elder.

Eternity passed before they finally broke away from each other, Donovan with a smirk and Nadine with flushed cheeks.

"Donovan and I are a match. He is actually my only match."

"Right … the matching process the Grand Elder mentioned," I replied.

"Did you hear about your matches?" Donovan asked as he snaked an arm around Nadine's shoulder, tugging her into his side.

"Not yet."

Even though he had Nadine glued to his side, his eyes bored straight into mine. There was something in them. I wasn't sure what. I didn't really want to find out.

"I'm excited to hear about who you get matched with. I heard about our little last-minute swap." He trailed his eyes down my body.

"Nadine, we should probably go," I mumbled, taking a few more steps, putting me back in the hallway and out of the dark room. With a smirk on his face, he nudged Nadine forward and into the hallway.

"Yes, Nadine, show our new friend around," he chimed, as he closed the door in our faces.

She latched on to my arm, wrapping herself around it as she spilled about her dates with Donovan. Nadine was in high spirits. Her higher pitch gave her away. I was happy for her. She genuinely looked as if she liked Donovan. But I was concerned for her.

He was a man who looked like he had secrets.

CHAPTER 14

S leep once more evaded me. I stared at the wall my bed was pushed against. For every somewhat decent vampire I met, there was one equally frightening. The verdict was still open on the silver-haired man and Amelia, but they were far better than the Grand Elder and Donovan.

With a big stretch, I rolled out of bed. No point in dwelling longer in bed. I needed to get my blood drawn before I would be able to officially start my day. After that, I would be free to do whatever I pleased, which meant sitting in the gathering room since we weren't allowed to roam the castle freely,—only the gathering room, the nurse's office, and our own bedrooms.

The cold floor pressed against my feet. If I finished up at the nurse's office early, I might be able to beat Nadine to the gathering room. It was hard to talk to the other girls when she was around because no one wanted to be in her company. But I felt obligated to stay with her; she was the only one who truly attempted to get to know me.

With my feet on autopilot, it didn't take long to arrive at the nurse's office. I knocked on the door, waiting for the okay to enter. Yesterday, I didn't have time to ask a lot of questions, so today was the day to finally learn more about my new home.

"Come in!" Amelia's voice chimed through the door, and I pushed it open. Just like before, she was sat at her desk scribbling away on some papers, not bothering to look up. Her office was still the same as when I was here yesterday. I was doing my best trying to remember things about the castle, which wasn't too hard when my access was limited to three rooms.

"Good morning, Veronica. I didn't take you for an early riser," Amelia said as she stood from behind her desk

"It was the first day," I grumbled, as I made my way over to an empty exam table.

There was already another girl in the room sitting on an exam table waiting to have her blood drawn. Amelia made her way over to us, starting with the girl who was already there.

Like all the other girls, she wore a dress that was similar, but hers was a pale green, which complemented her tanned skin and curly brown hair. Her eyes flicked my way briefly, widening as we made eye contact, then she went back to looking out the window. My eyes narrowed, a knot forming in my belly at her display. I had a feeling it was because I hung out with Nadine, but I couldn't be too sure.

Before I could question the girl in the green dress, Amelia said, "All set. You are free to leave." With no time wasted, the girl bolted out of the nurse's office.

"All right, Veronica, it's your turn," Amelia said as she got to work on my arm, but I lingered, looking at the door for a moment longer.

I wanted to make friends with the other girls to find out more about this place, but if this was going to be their reaction when I was nearby, it was going to be difficult.

"I have some good news for you today." Amelia's voice lifted a tone higher in her excitement.

"What would that be?" I drawled out, finally tearing my eyes from the door and back to the nurse, who was poking my arm with a needle.

"We already have a few matches."

"Already?" My voice cracked. The process to find a match was fast. "To who?"

The number of vampires I'd had the chance to meet so far was small.

"I can't say."

"Why can't you?"

"It's up to the matches if they want to make contact or not."

"Can you tell me anything? I wish I knew more about this place and what to expect."

Amelia's fingers paused, before finishing up the work on my arm. She turned to her tray to set her items down and organize, all the while not looking at me. "Understandable, since you were a last-minute change. For your questions, I can only answer a few." Her voice was low, but I heard it. "But be quick with it." This time when she spoke, she turned to face me, her eyebrows drawing together.

"I am to form a personal bond with my matched?"

"It depends on the one you match. The bond can vary from something platonic to more."

"How many matches do I have?"

"A few," she answered, causing me to frown. At least it was more than one, but I wasn't sure how many more though.

"And what happens if I don't get matched?" I asked.

Nadine wasn't able to tell me, other than *They went away*. But she didn't know exactly what that meant and I was intent on finding out. Amelia stood, her arms crossing over her chest as she paced in front of me. Dread formed in my stomach. Not being matched was starting to look like a terrible thing.

"To not be matched … is dangerous."

"Dangerous?" I blurted out.

"To not be matched means you have nothing to offer. And having nothing to offer means there is no reason to keep you around."

"So they will send me back home?"

"Back home? Never."

The meeting with the Grand Elder popped in my head. He'd mentioned that some girls would return home. But if I had to choose between believing him or Amelia, the nurse seemed like the more truthful source.

"Then where do they go if not home?"

"I think that's enough questions." Her eyes bored into mine as she nodded toward the door.

She wanted me to leave, but I still wanted answers. I hopped off the exam table and grabbed her hand.

"Please, I need to know what happens next." My voice was laced with desperation. I needed answers.

"To be matched means you are someone's personal blood bank, so you are protected. To not be matched means you don't have that protection, understand?"

I didn't. Amelia placed her hands on my shoulders and ushered me to the door. She was done. I would have to wait till tomorrow to see if I could get more answers out of her. There was one thing for certain though: something dangerous was going on in this castle and it all revolved around being matched.

"Veronica…" Amelia nudged me into the hallway. Her hand was on the door as she started to close it behind me. "If you want any chance of survival, you must be matched," she uttered, the door closing a second later.

I froze, her advice replaying in my mind. If I didn't already have an inkling that something dangerous was going on, Amelia's warning cemented it. I still didn't know what lurked in the darkness of the castle, but if I wanted to live, then I needed to find my match.

But first, I needed to find out who exactly I'd matched with.

Chapter 15

"Are you excited?" Nadine said beside me on one of the many pillows in the gathering room. Several other girls were in the room as well, but they kept their distance. Upon arrival from the nurse's office, she had been so excited to share that today I would find out who my matches were, for whoever was our match would be coming to collect us today. That was … if they wanted to meet us. The choice was theirs.

The door to the gathering room opened, drawing me from my thoughts. Excitement bubbled up as I sat up straighter, waiting for whoever was on the opposite side of the door to enter. But that excitement died and was replaced with dread, for I instantly recognized the man who entered—his green eyes filled with emotion, a smirk on his face as he strolled straight up to Nadine and me.

"Donovan! What are you doing here? I wasn't expecting you till later," Nadine exclaimed as she jumped from her pillow to latch on to his arm.

Not even a moment later, he had his lips on her with an audience to see. He wrapped his arm around her waist, tugging her into his body. A blush spread across my face as I looked away. Were they always going to be like this?

Then Donovan's deep voice floated in the air: "I'm actually here for Veronica."

I jerked my head up. Eyes wide, I took in Donovan's smirk and the confusion on Nadine's face as they both looked at me. He let his arm fall from Nadine's waist and stretched it out to me, waiting for me to grab his hand. My body stood rigid as Nadine adopted a frown, casting her eyes down to the floor.

"It's not polite to keep one waiting," he said, taking a step forward, causing me to take a step back.

"Veronica, you should go…" Nadine whispered. "After all, you are matched."

I stared at Donovan wide-eyed, my breathing rapidly increasing. *We were matched?* Today was the day we would meet our matches, and Donovan had come for me. He was one of my matches. Dread filled inside as he grasped my hand, yanking me right into his chest; his hand wrapped around my waist. He waved goodbye to the rest of the girls as he led me out of the gathering room.

"Where are we going?" I asked, grimacing as his hand tightened on my waist.

"It's a surprise. Just wait, I promise it will be magical."

"Why can't Nadine come?" My question caused him to pause. His green eyes bored into mine and I looked away, unable to stare back.

"Because I want alone time with you."

He started the trek down the hallway once more, me glued to his side. He led us to a spiral staircase in a circular room. On the opposite side were the doors that led outside. On the other side of the doors was the area where I'd first arrived. It felt like a lifetime, but it was only a few days ago that I 'd stolen away from home in order to let my sister marry the love of her life.

I focused back to the stairs as we started our walk up, but my attention was drawn to how the steps continued down as well. This wasn't the first floor. There was something under the castle.

I peered down in an attempt to see anything, but all that greeted me was darkness.

Donovan continued up the stairs. I was forced to follow, only stopping after we'd taken five flights of stairs. A jerk to the right —and a huge smile shot in my direction from Donovan—had us going down another hallway. Whatever was on this floor was the magical surprise he'd spoken of just moments ago.

"Donovan, where are we going?" I pressed once more, the unease still inside me with every step we took.

"Right up there!" he exclaimed, one hand pressed tightly on my waist as his other pointed to a door coming up.

But it was the door that was barely cracked open to my right that had my eyes growing wide. Inside were a few girls huddled close, none of the luxuries in the gathering room present in this one. They were huddled together, but it was the girl in the center that drew my attention. She was the spitting image of the girl in the nurse's office who wore a pale green dress. But this one wore a dark green dress.

I tugged at Donovan, trying to get him to release his hold on me so I could go to the room, ask the girls what they were doing and why they were there. But Donovan was having none of it and the room fell farther away.

"Here we are!" he exclaimed, opening the closed door, the rush of cool air against my skin drawing my attention back to Donovan.

A chill coursed through my body. The dresses we were forced to wear did little to provide cover against the elements.

"This is one of my favorite spots in the castle," Donovan said as he unwound his arm from around my waist and stepped outside.

The ledge was wide enough that a few people could stand on it together, but that was it. One wrong step and one would find themselves crashing to the ground.

He reached out, grabbing my own hand at my side, not waiting for me to take a hold of it, and tugged me out onto the ledge. I gasped as I pressed myself to the castle, putting as much distance between myself and the edge as possible.

"Don't worry, I got you."

That was exactly why I was worried. Donovan didn't scream *trustworthy*; and to be out on the ledge with no barrier was a recipe for disaster. I had no other choice; he tugged on my hand. I joined Donovan out further on the ledge.

"Live life on the edge!" he shouted, following it with a laugh.

I grimaced at his attempt at a joke. From high on the ledge, I could look down into the line of trees that covered the grounds. Some of them reached the height of the floor we were on. For us to be above the canopy, the distance between each floor must be huge. A huge gust of wind sent me tumbling forward, attempting to grasp on to something to help settle my balance. But all that got me was Donovan's hand wrapped around my waist as he brought me close to his chest. His green eyes stared down into mine.

Donovan was a man who seemed to find an excuse to be close with someone. "Breathtaking, isn't it?" His eyes drifted to something between the trees.

Curiosity piqued, I too looked in the direction he was to see what had captured his eye. My breath hitched, for hidden in the trees was a lake. It reminded me of home, one of my own favorite spots to go and escape reality.

"Wow…" I mumbled.

"That isn't the only breathtaking thing out here."

I knew he wasn't talking about something out in nature, for his words were hot against my ear. He was talking about me. Refusing to fall for his antics, I unwrapped myself from him and kept my eyes trained on the lake.

"Come. I set up a little picnic for us to enjoy." He shuffled away from me.

With no choice but to follow him, I trailed after him farther out on the ledge, where a blanket and a basket came into view.

"Hope this is suitable for a first date," he said as he sat on the blanket, patting the empty space, beckoning me to join him.

I joined him on the blanket, doing my best to keep my back pressed against the wall and my feet far from the edge. The exact opposite of Donovan, who had his feet hanging over the ledge freely. Nerves bumbled inside as he stared at me.

"I wasn't sure what you liked, so I got a few things in here."

He rifled through the basket by his side. Two plates of food, one with sandwiches already pre-cut to make for easy eating. The other was a bowl of mixed fruit. The last thing he pulled out were two wine glasses. He handed me my glass.

"Excuse me one moment," he muttered, setting down his own glass before getting up.

He stepped over my legs to go back into the hallway to grab whatever he might have forgotten. The brief break from Donovan allowed me to breathe easier. But it was only a moment before he reappeared with two bottles in hand. Once more, he stepped over me to his position on the other side of the blanket. With ease, he popped open the first bottle and poured some in my glass. I brought the glass up to my nose and sniffed, instantly recognizing the smell of wine. Did he truly expect me to drink while we sat on a ledge high above the ground?

The opening of the second bottle drew my attention, for the bottle wasn't the same as the one just opened. Was his intention for each of us to have a bottle of our own to drink? I looked closely at the bottle in his hand that had no label. A bright red liquid oozed out as he poured it into his glass. It didn't flow like my drink.

"That doesn't look like wine."

"I would offer you some, but you don't seem like the type to drink blood," he said, followed by a laugh.

He wasted no time in bringing the glass to lips and taking a long drink from it, despite my mouth dropping open. I knew vampires drank blood. That was the whole reason we were here: to find a match so we could become their personal blood bank. There was just something different about actually seeing someone drink blood that unsettled me. It made everything real.

Donovan downed his glass in no time and refilled it, bringing the glass to his lips once more. Nausea formed as I watched him to the point that if I kept looking I would surely throw up. I dragged my eyes from the man beside me to the lake, wishing I was out there by the water, instead of up here next to him.

"I hope everything is to your liking."

"It's not bad," I mumbled.

It was an overstatement. This was not my ideal type of date. Stuck on a ledge with a man I felt I couldn't trust.

"Not bad? Well, I guess I will just have to do better for the second date."

My skin crawled. I knew there was a smirk growing on his face without even having to look. He let loose a low chuckle, and the feeling of dread was back. Donovan was someone I didn't want to go on a second date with.

CHAPTER 16

"You've been spending a lot of time with Donovan lately," Nadine said, refusing to look in my direction, opting instead to keep her head toward the ground.

"I don't see Donovan in any sort of romantic way. You can have him when it comes to that," I replied.

"Are you sure?"

"Absolutely."

"Thank you! You're the best," she exclaimed, wrapping her arms around my shoulders as she flung herself on me.

I didn't know why she would like a man like Donovan. He didn't have any charming qualities except his green eyes. That was something I could admit to. My eyebrows drew together as I rubbed Nadine's back. The fact she thought I was interested in Donovan was worrying. She raised her head, a smile on her face and a twinkle in her eye. She was happy that I wasn't interested in Donovan romantically. I don't even think I could see Donovan as a friend.

"By chance, are you hanging out with him today?" Her once excited voice was quieter now.

"I think so. He is the only one to come for me for so far," I replied.

Nadine unwrapped herself from me, going back to her own seat beside me. I wasn't interested in Donovan, but the fact I still had to spend time with him unsettled her. There was nothing I could do. If he came for me, I had to go.

My breath hitched as the door to the gathering room opened. I tried to still my rapidly beating heart. Every time I saw Donovan he invoked responses in me that I couldn't control, and they weren't the good responses of seeing someone of the opposite sex. But this time, it wasn't Donovan with his dark hair and green eyes who strolled in. It was a man with blond hair and striking blue eyes, as bright as the sky. His frame was tall, and on the skinny side, the opposite of Donovan's bulky frame. He smiled, showing his pearly white teeth as he scanned the area, looking for whoever he'd come to retrieve. I sighed; the man wouldn't be here for me. The only one who came to get me was Donovan. It seemed it would be that way for a while. I wouldn't put it past the man to scare away my other matches. I just had to be content watching the new guy as he entered the room looking around.

My heart sped up when his eyes landed on mine. He turned in my direction, walking straight towards Nadine and me. My heart couldn't take it, it felt like it was going to burst, for this man was a dream, total opposite of the vampires I had met so far. Everyone had darkness around them, especially the Grand Elder and Donovan, but this man? Felt like he oozed light, as if he were surrounded by sunshine. He stopped right in front of us. A part of me thought he must be confused, there was no way he was here for me. As if my wish were granted, he sent my heart into a frenzy.

"Veronica, correct?" he asked, his voice light as he brought his hand up to run it through his blond locks.

Everything about him was a contrast, and I was drawn in immediately. I nodded in response as I examined him finally, given the chance at our close proximity. His skin was flushed, not even a hint of gray like the Grand Elder. No deep bags on his face and, of course, that smile … a smile that caused my heart to flutter.

"Well, Veronica, it seems we have been matched," he said once more, extending his hand out to me.

Unlike Donovan, he waited for me to grasp his hand before pulling me up from my seat on the floor.

"I know you're supposed to hang out with Donovan today, but I figured I should sneak you away before I lost the chance."

"Sneak me away to where? And who are you?" I asked.

I could feel the eyes of the other girls in the room on us. My cheeks flushed. Could they see how drawn I was to the man?

"I'm Alexander, and I think it's time we had our first date." His fingers entwined with mine as he led the way out of the gathering room.

I turned to look back at Nadine, to make sure she would be okay by herself, but I didn't have to worry because she was waving me on, urging me to go with Alexander, mouthing *Good luck*. Good luck with what? It was just a first date.

"I didn't think my second match would show up," I said as he led the way down the hallway.

"It's up to us if we decide to show ourselves. Figured I was done waiting, so here I am. I hope you aren't disappointed."

"Absolutely not," I muttered, but it wasn't low enough. He laughed as he shot a look over his shoulder in my direction.

My cheeks heated even more for being caught. I was glad I didn't have to spend the day with Donovan, but I was even more excited to get to know the man before me.

"I have a surprise planned. Nothing as exciting as Donovan's, but still a surprise nonetheless."

I nodded, but he couldn't see as he kept his eyes trained ahead. Just like with Donovan, we went up the staircase, but unlike before we didn't stop on the fifth floor. My eyes drew to the door that contained the girls as we passed. This time it was shut and I couldn't see anything as we continued up.

"How many floors are there in the castle?"

"Technically nine, but things stop on the eighth floor. Which is exactly where we are going."

His answer brought a smile to my face. No pushback, no vague answer. He had answered with no hesitation. If it was going to be like this, him being open to sharing, then I would gladly spend every day with Alexander.

"There isn't many of us on this floor. Just a few of us."

He led me down the hallway to the left of the stairs. On the wall were pictures of vampires. The one I recognized instantly was the portrait of the Grand Elder. But it was the one beside him that had my eyes going wide, for it was the man I was with. Alexander was on the wall!

"Here we are!" he blurted out, pulling me from my thoughts as we arrived in front of dark wooden double doors. He let go of my hand to push open the doors, allowing me a full view of the room. It could be described in one word, and that was breathtaking.

The room was a bedroom fit for a king. In the center was a black velvet couch accompanied by two chairs around a table. In the center of the sitting arrangement was a simple coffee table with a few items on it. But it was what lay beyond the sitting area that was memorizing, for it was a wall of windows.

"What is this room?" I asked as I took a step in. Now that I had entered, I could see a bed a bit farther behind the sitting area.

"It's my bedroom. I hope you don't mind," he said, as he maneuvered in front of me, looking sheepish. "We can go somewhere else if it's too awkward."

"No, it's okay," I muttered as I inched forward into the room. The sun blasted into the room, bathing everything in its light. No wonder Alexander radiated warm vibes if this was his bedroom.

"Have a seat while I pour us a glass." He turned to a cabinet right next to the door.

He pulled out two glasses and a bottle, popping it open. I couldn't see what he was pouring; his back blocked my view. All I could do was wait to see what he brought out. There were several places to sit, but if I sat on the couch, there was a good chance he might sit next to me. My heart might be too weak for that, so one of the chairs would do. As soon as I sat down, Alexander turned with two glasses in hand.

A smile spread across my face, for it wasn't wine. But the shocking part was that it was two glasses of champagne and not a single glass of blood. Being surrounded by vampires was still a new thing, and having Donovan openly drink blood next to me was a first. I wasn't sure if it was actually something I could sit next to every day as if everything were normal.

"Champagne?" he asked as he extended a glass to me.

My hand lingered a moment too long on his as I grasped the glass.

"I thought champagne would be a safe bet, so I am glad you like it," he said, as he turned to sit on the couch.

Upon sitting, he got comfortable, crossing his legs and resting one arm on the armrest.

"I like … but I admit, I thought you would be drinking something else."

His laugh filled the air, causing my face to heat up.

He knew exactly what I was talking about. "I drink blood because I have to. But I prefer to have the human alternatives for things as much as possible."

I looked at Alexander in a different light. We'd met only moments ago, but he was different. I could feel it. He was a light in the darkness of the castle, and I wanted to cling to it for dear life. I wanted Alexander to be my match.

"I hope you don't mind spending the day with me."

"Do we have anything planned?"

"Just talking, if you don't mind."
I didn't, not one bit.

Chapter 17

I sighed as I once more found myself outside the nurse's office, waiting to have my daily blood draw. The past few days had been bliss. I was on cloud nine, I would even dare to say. There were moments I had to spend with Donovan, but the majority of it was spent with Alexander. He was consuming a lot of my time, but he was consuming my mind every moment.

"Come in!" Amelia's voice chimed through the door, granting me access to her office.

It was a routine I was very familiar with as I strolled forward to the exam table. A few pricks in the arm and I would be all set to leave and wait for whoever would come to get me today. My face felt hot as I thought about spending another day with Alexander.

"I guess you aren't an early riser anymore," Amelia said, a smirk on her face.

"The last few days have been busy."

"Yes … I've heard about you and Alexander." She wheeled herself over to my side on the stool she sat on.

My face was already hot, but it was increasing. I looked down at my feet. It was no secret. I was sure people could tell I was becoming smitten with Alexander. But for Amelia to know about it, that meant Alexander had to be talking about me. And if he was talking about me, then there was a good chance he also liked me.

"He wasn't what I was expecting to find here."

"I'm not surprised. Alexander clings to reminders of his human life," she answered as she prepped my arm.

"What is it like to be a vampire?" I asked.

Her fingers paused on my arm only briefly before continuing their task.

"Why do you ask?"

"I'm just curious. There are so many things about this place I don't understand. I feel like in order to truly understand, I need to know more about being a vampire."

"There isn't much to discuss."

"Surely there is something you can tell me. There has to be a difference from being a human to being a vampire."

She continued her task in silence. I didn't want to press her, but with her role as a nurse that catered to both humans and vampires, she would know everything there was to know about the differences between our kinds.

"I really shouldn't be telling you information. You also shouldn't be asking questions."

Should I bite my tongue? I stared at the wall ahead. I wasn't trying to get her in trouble, but me knowing nothing would not help me in the long run. There was so much about the castle and its residents that I didn't know.

"But I like you, Veronica. One of the few that actually think."

My embarrassment grew. I kept my eyes on the wall ahead. She considered me one of the few that thought. It could be seen as both a compliment and an insult. If that was the criteria to have her share information, then I would see it as a good thing.

"Does that mean you'll tell me more about your kind?"

"Again, there isn't really anything exciting about us. We need blood to live and we get it from those who are offered to us."

"What about special abilities?" I asked.

"Like flying or something?" she managed to say in between in her laughs.

My embarrassment skyrocketed. It was a reasonable question to ask—at least I thought so. The castle gates closed on their own, so there was some type of magic somewhere.

"No, we don't fly."

"So vampires are just regular humans who drink blood?"

"Basically. We do have enhanced senses and traits. So someone who was strong when they were human is stronger as a vampire."

My mouth dropped. Amelia was speaking as if vampires were truly equal to humans. But a strong human was an even stronger vampire, and that wasn't normal.

"Everyone has enhanced senses?"

"For the most part. At least one enhanced sense or maybe two. Strength isn't my forte, so I'm not enhanced in that area. I'm actually considered pretty weak on vampire terms. Donovan, who I'm sure you're familiar with, is really strong. But I got him beat in the knowledge department."

A chuckle escaped me. I had to agree, for while Donovan was strong, he did seem to have a one-track mind, which always revolved around females or blood. It was always one or the other. But it wasn't Donovan I was curious about. There was specifically someone with blond hair and bright blue eyes.

"What about Alexander?"

"It seems someone is developing a crush," she joked, and my face heated up. There was just something about Alexander that brought warm, fuzzy feelings inside.

"I would say he's average. He doesn't really lean one way or the other, most likely due to him not really embracing his vampire side."

Ease and relief settled inside. I didn't have to worry about Alexander going crazy with super strength or something. We could just be normal together in a castle filled with abnormal people. It was already the impression I got from him, one he even communicated. But hearing it from someone else was comforting. It would strengthen my feelings that Alexander was the one I wanted to be matched with, and I would do anything to have that happen.

"You are all set. You can head back to the gathering room, Veronica." She wheeled herself away from my side and back to her desk, where once situated she got straight to work writing on some papers.

I stared at Amelia for a moment longer, but she'd checked out. There would be no more questions for today. I would have to wait for tomorrow.

A light knock on the door drew me out of my thoughts as I jumped off the exam table. Another girl was probably here to get her blood drawn, and I had to get back to the gathering room where, hopefully, Alexander would come for me once more.

Luck was on my side, for the door cracked opened and a head of blond hair with bright blue eyes peeked in. A smile instantly formed on both of our faces when our eyes met. Instead of waiting for me to return to the gathering room, he'd come to retrieve me. We both couldn't wait to see each other.

"What are you doing here?"

Amelia glanced up from her paperwork. She wasn't annoyed at the interruption, the smirk on her face giving her away.

"I came to see if Veronica was up for hanging out again," Alexander started.

"I'm sure she would be delighted," Amelia answered, being totally right that I would be, but it didn't mean she needed to embarrass me.

I scurried to the doors as quickly as possible, ushering Alexander back into the hallway and away from Amelia's watching eyes. I let loose a sigh, sagging as I shut the door behind us, escaping further teasing at the hands of the nurse.

"I take that as a yes?" Alexander said beside me, causing me to look up into his bright blue eyes, a smile still on his face. It was almost a permanent fixture, or maybe only when we hung out. A girl could certainly dream. He laughed as he grabbed my hand, pulling me to his side as we walked down the hallway.

"Where to today?" I asked.

It didn't really matter where we were going. I would follow him anyway.

"I think a breath of fresh air will do us well. Unless you wanted to do something else?"

"No, that sounds perfect." And it did. Any time spent with Alexander would be wonderful. He was the light in this dark and dreary castle. He led us straight to the main entrance, where the stairwell that proceeded both up and down was located.

"Wait right here! I'll just be a moment," Alexander exclaimed, letting go of my hand as he ran up the stairs, taking two at a time.

My attention was divided away from watching him scale the stairs to a laugh that filled the hallway. A very familiar laugh.

I looked over my shoulder to see the head of red hair that belonged to Nadine. But it was the person who'd made her laugh that had my heart beating fast. I wanted to shrink away and hide in a corner. Arm wrapped around, her body was tightly pressed against Donovan. He must have sensed me looking, his green eyes leaving Nadine's and meeting mine. A frown graced his face as he headed in my direction. I couldn't run and hide, because then I would not be here when Alexander descended the stairs, and I wanted to be.

Alexander had been consuming more and more of my time, leaving me very little with Donovan. I wasn't complaining, but by the way Donovan walked with such passion in his steps, he didn't like it.

Footsteps descending the stairs drew my attention away until the blond hair of Alexander came into view. I leaped up the stairs, meeting his descent, latching on to his arm, and he almost dropped the coats he'd retrieved. A smile spread across my face as he was thrown off for a second. I was happy. He was a Prince Charming who always arrived at the right moment.

I ushered him down the stairs quickly and straight out the doors to the outside. A side glance thrown Donovan's way had me seeing he'd paused, both him and Nadine looking at us, one in happiness and the other one in annoyance.

"It might be a bit chilly outside, so I brought you a coat that will help keep you warm." Alexander lifted the biggest jacket from his arms to drape over my shoulders. I quickly shoved my arms into the sleeves, and warmth radiated into me as I clutched the coat close. It was bulky and not the most flattering for my body, but it was a cocoon of warmth, which was much needed with the simple dresses we were forced to wear.

Being able to go outside was nice after being locked up in the castle for days, a breath of fresh air away from all the things going on in the castle I wasn't privy to. Just on the other side of the door were Donovan and Nadine. Would they be coming outside as well? The thoughts of the two we had just run past died as Alexander stood in the other coat he'd brought—a long slender one that fit his frame. A big coat like mine would dwarf his body. His hand entwined with mine as he tugged us off the castle front entrance and onto the ground. The feeling of dirt underneath my feet, followed by crunching leaves, was welcome, a break from the cold stone floors of the castle.

"There is a small trail to the side we can walk."

I nodded, following on the trail after Alexander as he led the way. It was beautiful outside. The sun shone brightly on everything outside, lighting our path as we entered the trees.

Alexander picked up his speed, bringing it to a light jog, leaving me with no choice but to match his pace. His back was to me, leading the way, his jacket swaying in the wind with each step he took. He shot a smile over his shoulder and I returned it.

Followed by a laugh because I enjoyed every second with the man.

I had always wanted a happily-ever-after. There was a period where I thought Jax and I would be able to grow to love one another, but that was dashed by the confession from Rory. Swapping places with her left me with a lot of uncertainty. The only thing driving me at the time was making sure my sister could smile again. I hadn't known that I would find my own happiness within the castle in the arms of the blond man with blue eyes. Butterflies fluttered inside at the thought of what we could become. It was something I was looking forward to exploring.

Chapter 18

"A lexander! How much longer are we to run for?" I called out to him.

He was taking us a bit of distance away from the castle. He shot a smile in my direction, easing my worry that was forming.

"Really, Alexander?" I called once more, followed by a laugh.

Being with him was natural. Everything just felt right. It wasn't like we'd just met days ago but like I'd known him my whole life.

"We're almost there!" he called, turning slightly, allowing him enough room to tug me right into his chest.

With one of our hands still entwined, he snaked the other around my waist, bringing me close to his body. Never stopping our jog forward, he pressed on with me at his side. My cheeks grew hot at the close contact we shared. We were running into the unknown, but I would run anywhere with him by my side. A breath of fresh air, a light in the dark I was eager to hold on to, no matter what. Our pace finally slowed to a walk.

"We're here! A date outside!" he exclaimed, letting go of my hand to wave at the setup before us.

It seemed all the men thought picnics were the most romantic gesture there was, but it was the alone time it provided that I liked most. An escape from reality next to someone who unleashed butterflies inside—sorely lacking with the experiences of Jax and Donovan. We proceeded forward, a gasp getting caught in my throat. We weren't up on a ledge with a chance of falling to our death at any moment. Alexander had set up a picnic in a field of flowers.

"Do you like? You mentioned it previously, and I thought it would be a good idea. Especially since you haven't been having the best of luck with them."

"I love it. Thank you for replacing bad memories with good ones."

Once more, he entwined our hands together, leading the way through the bed of flowers, straight to the center, where our blanket was.

"Ladies first." He helped me down onto the blanket.

I didn't need it, but it was the simple thought of him taking care of me that created a permanent smile on my face. Everything about Alexander was different from the other men especially Donovan, and I was becoming completely smitten by him.

"I don't know everything you like, which I'm hoping will change soon. In the meantime, I did pack a few things for today," he said, motioning to the basket as he joined me on the blanket.

I cracked open the lid and peered inside. My eyebrows squished together, for what was inside were two books. Hesitantly, I reached inside, setting them on my lap. The books had no titles to give away what lay inside. I would have to see for myself. Picking up the first one, I opened to a random page and read about the history of vampires. I bit down on my lip as I opened the second book, which talked about humans.

"Are these history books?" I asked, peering up at Alexander, my eyebrows knitted together. Why history books on a date?

"In a way, yes. It's more like lore, but it does contain some truth."

He picked the up the vampire book, setting it back in my lap, while grabbing the human book to put in his.

"I figure since we should know more about each other, it would be good to understand and learn about our kind. You can ask me questions and get the truth straight from the source. Same for me if I have questions," he said, pulling at his collar, avoiding my gaze.

It wasn't a lavish gift, but it was one that had meaning behind it. So often I was frustrated at not understanding what was happening in the castle, and Alexander had picked up on it. He'd found a way to tell me by letting me ask questions while I read the book. But that wasn't all. He was also interested in learning more about humans.

I didn't take us as some mystery, but maybe we were just like how vampires are a mystery to me. Alexander still avoided my gaze, but I wanted him to know I appreciated the gift. Mustering up the courage and trying to not think about it too much, I leaned in, placing a quick kiss on his cheek before backing away.

"There is more in the basket," he said softly, his eyes now fully focused on me.

It was too much to stare back. It was the first time we had done anything but hold hands. Once more, I peered into the basket and pulled out a small cloth that contained something inside. A silver rectangle piece was exposed after carefully picking apart the cloth. I shot a look over at Alexander as I picked it up, inspecting it, realization dawning as I knew what it was.

"You know how to play this?" I asked, doubt laced in my voice.

"The harmonica is one of my favorites that I play." He reached across to grab the musical instrument from my hand.

"As in you play other instruments as well?"

"Of course," he said, as if it was unnatural to not play multiple instruments.

I had no idea how to play a single one. Alexander brought the harmonica to his lips and started to play. A soft tune swarmed around us as he brushed his lips across the harmonica, creating sweet melodies that instantly warmed me inside.

Ease crept into my body. I was unable to look anywhere but at the beautiful sight before me. His eyes closed while his lips and hands hard at work, creating magic in the air.

Alexander's head bobbed every so often, causing the wind to drift into his blond locks, giving life to them. He cracked an eye open, looking right at me, before closing it once more and continuing playing. In the presence of Alexander, everything was just so much more peaceful. It was as if the only thing that mattered was the two of us and there was nothing else in the world. Everything just made sense when I was by his side.

The music stopped as he removed the harmonica from his lips. A smile spread as heat rushed to my cheeks. He'd caught me staring at him, too memorized to look away.

"You look absolutely beautiful."

His words were music to my ears. It was nice to be looked at in that way. When everything before Alexander was going downhill, he was turning everything around.

"Keep looking. There are a few more items in there."

I nodded, still refusing to look up and meet his bright blue eyes and wonderful smile. I dug back into the basket before me. Already removed from the basket were books and a harmonica. What else did he have hidden away?

My fingers rubbed against a small box, and I brought it out so I could have a better look at it. Upon closer inspection and a little jingle, the contents had to be jewelry related. Had he already got me something when we barely knew each other?

My hands trembled as I opened the box and grabbed the piece inside. It was a black cloth choker, but the piece that stood out the most was the clasp in the middle that pinched the cloth together. On that clasp was a yellow gemstone that dangled off, forming the image of a sun with smaller gems creating rays.

"This is too much." I ran my finger over the gems. It had to have cost a decent amount of money to buy. Gems weren't cheap.

"Absolutely not," Alexander responded, grabbing the necklace from my hands. "You have really brightened up my day, and even though we haven't known each other long, I see you as my sun ... someone who I can count on to be a ray of light, especially when the castle is always so dark and gloomy."

Tears welled in my eyes. It was the exact way I saw him. He was the sun inside the darkness of the castle, a beacon of hope for the happily-ever-after I could have. The feelings bubbling inside were overwhelming. It was wonderful to hear he thought of me the same way I viewed him.

"Let me put it on you," he uttered as he rested on his knees.

I turned, grabbing a hold of my hair to allow easy access to my neck. His fingers brushed against my skin, sending jolts through my body. I did my best to control my reaction. After hearing him practically confess, it was extremely hard to be in control of my emotions.

The cloth was smooth, while the gem was cold like ice.

"All set! It suits you very well."

I turned back to him once more so he could see the necklace in its full glory.

"What kind of stone is this?"

"A sunset fire opal."

"A sunset fire opal…" I repeated after him, fiddling with the gem. It was a beautiful name for a stone just as beautiful. It resembled the burning embers of the sun.

"I'm afraid the only thing left in the basket is nourishments," Alexander said as he dug into the basket, pulling out a container.

I was glad there was just food left. Having more gifts bestowed upon me would be too much. I had nothing to offer in return, and if things were truly going to work between us, there had to be an equal balance of give and take.

I grabbed the vampire book, ready to dive in. Alexander handed me a bottle of juice. He opened his own and brought it to his lips for a sip.

"You look like you have a question," he asked, bringing the juice away from his mouth.

"You aren't drinking blood again," I blurted out.

"I drink blood, but correct, I am not drinking it now. Am I supposed to drink it all the time?" he asked, followed by a laugh.

"I just figured based on my limited interaction with vampires … Donovan drinks it all the time."

"Comparing me to Donovan? That is such a low bar I don't know whether to be offended or happy." He let loose a chuckle. "Donovan prefers to embrace his vampire side more than I. So yes, he does drink blood more than just out of necessity. I do it only because it is a requirement."

"Thank you for answering," I murmured softly, casting my gaze back to the book in my lap. Music filled the air once more as Alexander started to play—a sweet melody to match the mood of enjoying my time with Alexander.

CHAPTER 19

"How was your time with Alexander yesterday?" Nadine asked as she sat next to me in the gathering room.

I was still on cloud nine from being able to spend so much time with him. A breath of fresh air that I wanted to consume every moment. The sun necklace still rested against my skin as I fiddled with it, memories of the rest of the date with Alexander flooding my mind. A smile was going to be permanently on my face if I kept thinking of the blond-haired man with blue eyes.

"It was absolutely out of this world," I managed to say in between my sighs.

Nadine's laugh filled the air as she clutched onto my arm. "I'm so happy for you!"

"How was your time with Donovan?"

"Just like your time with Alexander. Absolutely amazing! Are you going to be hanging out with him today?"

"I hope so," I replied, for I wanted to spend every day with him.

The door to the gathering room creaking open drew my attention away from the red ball of hair to the front of the room.

"Ladies," a deep voice bellowed out, my body freezing in response.

It was Donovan who'd entered the room. He made his way to stand right in front of us, Nadine unlatching from me . She always got overjoyed when seeing him, to the point she jumped up and hooked onto him. He bent down and placed a quick kiss on her lips before turning away with her attached to his side.

As they walked toward the door to leave the gathering room, I was finally able to breathe. Before they crossed the threshold to go out into the hallway, Donovan paused. My stomach dropped as he smirked.

"Alex is busy, so you're with us today."

I flinched. It also didn't help that Nadine shot a look over her shoulder in my direction. I'd told her a thousand times that I wasn't interested in Donovan and that she could have him, but she still felt insecure when I was around him. If I could have my way, I would never be in his presence. I wanted all my time to be consumed by Alexander.

"Well, are you coming?" Donovan's deep voice once more filled the gathering room.

He made no move to take the final steps to enter the hallway and out of my sight. He was truly waiting for me to follow. I followed after them, my steps hesitant, wanting to instead run away.

We entered the hallway, Nadine still clutched to Donovan's side. I trailed a few paces behind. The direction we were heading was not toward the stairs. A sigh of relief escaped me; we weren't going to the ledge. It might have been Donovan's favorite place, but it was one step away from death, literally.

It also meant we weren't going to pass the room that I'd seen the girls in before. I'd meant to ask about them, but Donovan didn't seem like the person to tell his secrets. And when I was with Alexander, I forgot everything, too enchanted by his presence. It was hard to focus with his lips brushing against the harmonica, bringing sweet melodies to life, his blue eyes observing every movement I made. My cheeks grew hot as I tried to shake thoughts of Alexander from my mind.

"Hurry up, Veronica, we don't have all day to waste!" Donovan exclaimed, his sharp tone cutting through the air, pulling me from my thoughts and back to the present.

Both Donovan and Nadine stood in front of a door. I hadn't been to this part of the castle before, so what lay behind was a mystery. Not wanting to invoke his ire more, I followed behind. I briefly closed my eyes from the onslaught of steam that blasted into my face upon entry.

"Why are we here?" I questioned as I observed the room we were in.

It was a large bathroom, and unlike the one in the gathering room, this one had a giant communal tub of water in the center, big enough to fit at least ten people comfortably.

"It's a bathhouse. It should be easy to determine what we're doing in here." He made his way over to showers that lined one side of the room.

Obviously, a bath would be used to freshen up, but that didn't explain why there was a giant one in the center, and the three of us in the same room. Nadine followed after Donovan, using the shower stall next to him as they started to undress.

I cast my eyes away, unable to look at them as the water started to run. They might not be fazed by sharing a bathroom together, but I was. Undressing next to Nadine was one thing, but having Donovan in the room was a different story. Steam rose from the water in the room, and all I could think was that I would rather be on the ledge than in here.

"Really, Veronica?" Donovan said, drawing my eyes back over to the voice. He had his head poked out from the shower, but thankfully the steam radiating from his stall blurred his body where it stuck out.

"If you don't shower, I'm going to be forced to have you shower with me. Unless that is what you wanted all along," he said, a smirk growing on his face.

That wasn't what I wanted, so I hauled it over to the farthest shower from them and closed the small curtain attached to it, something both of the other occupants had opted out of using. The showers clicking off had me pausing, waiting to hear what happened next.

Wet feet against the floor, followed by a splash. A frown graced my face. The whole intention of us being in this room was to share the bath together.

"Are you going to stay in there forever?" Donovan's deep voice called out.

If I could just hide out in here, I would, but his earlier comment about him joining me was something I didn't want. The shower stall could fit one, but fitting two would be a tight squeeze. Body parts would have to mash against body parts.

I stood on my tippy-toes to look over the shower wall, and indeed both Donovan and Nadine were in the center, soaking in the large expanse of water.

I groaned. I had no other choice than to join them. Discarding my clothes and bunching them to the side so they wouldn't get wet, I turned on the water and started to rinse. If I could be in the opposite corner from them, then I might survive today. Nadine could keep him occupied and I would just be the third wheel.

"Veronica, you should really join us..." His voice was low, and I knew I was testing his patience.

"Are we to be here all day?" I called out as I turned the shower off, reaching my hand past the curtain to grab a towel.

"Until I decide to leave."

I exited the shower, towel wrapped around my body. Just as I'd suspected, Nadine and Donovan were snuggled up in the water, his arms stretched out on the stone while Nadine leaned into his chest. I let a sigh escape. I didn't really see what she saw in him. If anything, she should be running the other way to find a guy like Alexander. I grabbed another towel before walking over to the water, towel still wrapped around my body as I dipped into the water on the opposite side of the bath than them, the second towel beside me on the stone for when it was time to leave so I wouldn't be fully exposed.

My body relaxed, the heat doing wonders, but the tension returned, as a pair of green eyes were glued on me. If only those green eyes could morph into the baby blue eyes of Alexander; the dark hair into blond. Then I would willingly venture to the other side of the water, but it was all an illusion. The man in the water nothing like Alexander.

"Veronica … you are supposed to be in the bath without the towel." His words had me clutching my cloth tighter to my body.

"I don't feel that comfortable," I replied, casting my gaze somewhere else so I wouldn't have to see the green eyes drift their sights under the water's surface.

It felt like an eternity until I felt the eyes drift away from me, the chatter between Donovan and Nadine filling the awkward silence in the room. It finally allowed me to relax. With a sigh of relief, I sagged against the wall, finally letting the heat of the water untie the knots in my body. I wondered what Alexander was doing today that caused me to get stuck with Donovan. The blond-haired man appeared in my mind once more, and almost instinctively I reached for the necklace around my neck. It was a staple in my limited wardrobe, a gift from Alexander I would forever cherish.

"Alex gave you that necklace?"

I clutched the necklace as I looked at Donovan, giving him a nod in reply. I didn't trust myself to reply, for I might spill just how important this necklace had become to me. A precious gift I didn't want to lose.

"Alexander may be the son of the Grand Elder but he doesn't have any power," Donovan exclaimed as he cupped Nadine's face, leaning in to place a kiss on her lips—which she hungrily replied to, pressing deep into his body. The scene unfolding in front of me didn't faze me. I was still trying to come to terms with his words.

The man who shone as bright as the sun, the one who was the light in this dark castle, was related to the man of my nightmares? How was that even possible? They were so vastly different, one with light hair and bright blue eyes and the other with darkness etched across every part of his body. I stared at Donovan as he broke away from Nadine for a moment, before leaning back in for another kiss. Alexander had no power despite his position. Why would that matter? What did one need power within the castle for?

As if reading my mind, Donovan cracked open an eye to look my way. His single green eye was joined by the other as he broke away from Nadine. She whimpered at the loss of contact and nuzzled her face into his neck, but his sole attention had turned to me, a smirk growing on his face as he leaned toward me, almost teasingly, as if he was going to cross the bath to me —it had me shrinking back, pressing myself against the stone.

"If I want you, I will have you. There is nothing Alexander can do about it."

CHAPTER 20

"**I**'m sorry that I wasn't there for you yesterday," Alexander said, his hand entwined with mine as we made our way up the stairs to his bedroom.

"Donovan mentioned you had something come up."

"I did," he replied.

A sigh escaped for his lack of explanation of what had pulled him away. But there were probably duties he had to attend to. After all, he was the son of the Grand Elder.

His hand squeezed mine as he shot me a smile. "I have something special planned," he exclaimed, increasing our speed up the stairs so we could reach his floor quicker.

"Are you going to share any details?" I pressed.

He always had something special planned, so I wasn't too surprised.

"Why would I do that?" he shot back, causing me to laugh, a smile forming as his mere presence made my heart flutter.

All I wanted was to spend every moment with Alexander, forgetting about the world around us.

"Why are you smiling?" he asked, only pausing briefly before we continued our way up the stairs.

"I'll tell you why I'm smiling when you tell me what you have planned for us."

"Well, then keep smiling because I'm not telling," Alexander replied, followed by a laugh as he held my hand tighter.

We finished the last steps to be on the floor of his bedroom and made a beeline straight to his door. I wasn't sure what the surprise was, but I wouldn't have to wait long to find out. If the surprise was simply being able to spend time with him, then I would be content.

"Surprise is in the box." He pulled open the doors to his bedroom, ushering me inside.

On the coffee table was a white package with a red ribbon wrapped around it. My fingers grasped the lid but I paused in opening the gift, as Alexander had turned around.

"Why did you turn around?"

He didn't provide a verbal response. He brought his hands up to his face to cover his eyes. He was already turned around. The additional coverage was just being extra. But it worked, for it piqued my interest. What was in the box? My attention back on the gift, I untied the ribbon and lifted the lid. My knees felt weak, my heart full of emotion at what lay in the package. The lid clattered to the ground as I grasped the item inside, lifting it up so I could see it in its full beauty. My cheeks grew wet as I took in the beauty in my hands.

"Are you crying? Do you not like it?" Alexander's voice was hesitant, and I hated he thought I would not like the gift he gave me, for in my hands was a gown of the silkiest gold fabric.

"No … I love it," I whispered, the tears flowing, unable to be contained; the sheer amount of happiness was overwhelming. "I'm to wear this?" I asked as I looked at Alexander, who still had his back to me. "Now?" I added as the realization dawned that he had his back turned because he expected me to get dressed.

"Absolutely!" he exclaimed, his happy voice bringing a smile to my face.

I wanted the day to continue, and in order for that to happen I needed to change. With a quick shimmy out of my current dress, which provided no resistance for it wasn't much cloth since it exposed so much, I stepped into the gold dress, pulling it up my legs, my smile growing and the tears increasing with every movement. The bottom of the dress cascaded out freely, creating a train. The bodice, though, was tighter than the skirt, a lot tighter. Upon closer inspection, it was a corset with the shoulder straps resting off my shoulders. It would allow the choker he'd gifted to have center stage. The thought Alexander put into everything had me almost collapsing to the floor from the overload of gratitude and happiness swarming inside.

I held the front of the dress to my chest as I reached back to zip it up, but was unable to. With heated cheeks, I looked to Alexander, who still had his back to me, and called out to him.

"Will you zip me up?"

His hands fell away from his face as he turned. My skin grew hot, watching his eyes widen as he made his way over to me. His mouth opened slightly several times, as if he wanted to speak but was rendered speechless. I looked into his bright blue eyes as he set his hands on my waist, a smile growing on his face. I never thought I would like getting dressed up but when it came to him, I would love everything.

"In order to zip you up, you will need to turn around," he whispered, his breath hot against my skin.

My body was already hot, but his comment made me embarrassed as I turned to expose my back to him. His hands shifted with my movement, never leaving my body. His fingers trailed to the zipper and drew it up slowly, the dress becoming tighter, conforming to my body as he did so. His touch lingered on my back before he stepped away, leaving me wanting to feel it once more.

"You look beautiful…" His voice was soft as he whispered.

I turned around to face him. "Thank you for the gift."

"I'm glad you wore the necklace." He reached out to grasp the pendent of the sun against my skin, his touch once more burning.

"One final thing."

"You don't need to get me anything."

"I swear it's the last thing," he replied as he grabbed something from his pants pocket and placed it in my hair.

I reached up to run my fingers across what was placed on my head, and a pattern of stones in a line could be made out. At the ends, it clipped into my hair, staying in place.

"Really, this is too much…"

"Nonsense. You deserve to be treated like a princess."

"What's all of this for?"

"A night of dancing," he replied, pulling me into his chest.

His smile grew as I wrapped my arms around him, and he started to sway us back and forth.

"But there's no music." It didn't really matter. I was spending time with Alexander and that was all that mattered.

But sooner or later, it would grow awkward with us just staring into each other's eyes, no matter how beautiful his were.

"I could hum a tune if you like." He didn't wait for a response. He started a soft hum to fill the silence.

Every moment spent with Alexander was the definition of perfect. A man so caring and attentive was only a pipe dream after everything with Jax, but finding a man who had eyes for me had feelings igniting inside. I leaned forward, placing my head on his chest, closing my eyes as he continued to sway back and forth. His humming never stopping for a moment.

"Is it true you're the son of the Grand Elder?" I blurted out, feeling my eyes widening. Why had I just ruined this perfect moment? But the words uttered by Donovan while in the baths rang in my ears. *If I want you, I will have you.* There was nothing Alexander could do.

"I am. Some would even say I'm a prince—one who has found his princess." A low chuckle escaped, before he continued humming once more.

"Donovan mentioned…"

"I don't want to talk about Donovan," Alexander said, cutting me off. "Won't you enjoy the here and now with me?"

His swaying had stopped, as had the soft hum from his lips. His bright blue eyes stared down at me as I stared back at him, seeing the frown on his face. He hadn't liked me bringing up Donovan, but I should have known better. It wasn't like I liked the green-eyed man, but I had unanswered questions—which would have to wait, for the moment between us was too wonderful to ruin.

A moment between us that I never wanted to end. Even one I dared say I wanted to explore more. Against all better judgment, the feelings swarming inside were too much to ignore, driving my urge, and I shut reason off, listening to my heart. I grasped his face, tilting him down to bring my lips to his. Before, the only intimacy had been a quick peck on the cheek, but I wanted more. The need to explore just how close Alexander and I could become was too great. His lips froze against mine, his bright blue eyes wide, causing me to panic for a moment.

But all the doubts disappeared as he tugged me close to his chest, his mouth urging mine to open. I responded eagerly. Before, when we were together, it was butterflies inside, but now it was as if nothing could be contained and feelings were pouring out.

His hand moved from my waist to the nape of my neck, running his fingers through my hair as he deepened the kiss. My knees grew weak, and I leaned on him for support as he finally broke away. My cheeks heated up at what had just transpired as he stared down at me, a smile on his face.

"I know you just put the dress on, but would you care if I removed it?"

Strong need fueled my response. His hands slid down my back, taking the zipper down so the dress was only held up by my chest pressing into his. If I wanted to stop, we could, for Alexander was a gentlemen, but I wanted this just as much as him. Maybe even more.

"Absolutely breathtaking."

A gasp escaped as his hand swooped under my thighs as he tilted me back so he could carry me. He leaned in once more, capturing my lips in a quick kiss, before proceeding to the bed. As gentle as his heart, he laid me on sheets, towering over me as he leaned once more, bringing his lips to mine. I reached up, my fingers running through his hair as I kept him close, never wanting him to part. But he had other plans. He broke the kiss, trailing light ones down my neck straight to my chest, stopping just above my dress.

He leaned in once more, capturing my lips in a quick kiss, bringing my dress down with his roaming hands. My body heated up, at first by embarrassment for being exposed, but that was quickly replaced by the need for more as he brought his mouth to enclose around my nipple. A slight tug had me winding my fingers through his hair, but it wasn't until his hand traveled lower that I gripped, bringing him close. Intense feeling so overwhelming I wanted to melt away brought on by the digit he slipped between the folds of my lower lips, my body igniting as another slipped in, his pace increasing.

"Alexander..." I mumbled between the gasps as he shook my very core, my free hand nestling into the bed sheets as I stared outside the window, the sun shining through, bathing the room in a glow.

My heart swelled with warmth not only because of the sun outside and its beauty but because of the sun I'd found inside the castle. A man who could make my heart flutter and knees weak with just one look, and certainty one lick.

My toes curled, back arching as I could feel the relief coming, the tension in my body too much. But with a few more thrusts, my essence shattered, my body crumbling into a heap as I tried to gather my breath, Alexander's blue eyes staring at me.

"Veronica…" His voice was low, lower than usual.

The simple uttering of my name after such an exchange of passion was enough to make me want to hold on and never let him go. The way he spoke my name unwound every fear, every worry that I could have had about my past and future to come.

"Veronica," he said once more as I mumbled out incoherent words.

I was still riding on cloud nine. I just needed a moment in order to collect myself.

"May I?" he asked, as I felt him shift beside me.

I nodded, but my eyes were closed so I wasn't entirely sure what he was asking. His chest pressed against mine, his lips now against my neck. A gasp escaped as his teeth pricked my skin, but it wasn't painful. It set my body on fire once more, sending me squirming underneath him, the need growing once more.

If this was what it was like to get bitten, then I had no problems being Alexander's personal blood bank.

CHAPTER 21

My body was still heated, Alexander's touch still lingering as I sat next to Nadine in the gathering room. Sleep didn't stay long, and there was no point lingering in bed daydreaming when I could get my day started and possibly see Alexander again. My cheeks felt hot as I touched them. The events of last night were ingrained in my memory. Being so recent, it was fresh too.

Nadine moving next to me drew my mind out of the cloud. I could tell she was mad at me, but for what was the question. She got up from her seat, leaving the gathering room, and headed in the direction of the nurse's office. With nothing else to do, I followed her. The amount of people I talked to in the castle could be counted on one hand. For her to ignore me meant that I was losing a good chunk of my social life.

"Nadine…" My voice came out as a whine.

Her pace, faster than normal, kept her a few steps ahead of me. Again, just like when I had greeted her when first coming to the gathering room, she ignored me. It would be hard to fix whatever was wrong between us if she wouldn't talk. I tried to think back to what could have happened to cause the rift, but my mind was blank—except for the image of a blond-haired man with striking blue eyes, but that had nothing to do with Nadine.

"Nadine!" I exclaimed, reaching out to her to grab hold of her arm.

We needed to settle this. It wouldn't do either one of us any good if we didn't at least try to talk about it. I was over having things snowball into a bigger issue like they'd done with Rory. At the time, I'd given up my wedding to be offered. This time, I wasn't sure what an alternative would be, and I certainly didn't want to find out.

"Nadine, please! Talk to me. What is going on?" I asked, my hand still firmly grasping her arm to prevent her from walking forward.

And it worked. She whirled on me, her red hair twisting, highlighting her face as if it were on fire, because it surely felt like it by the way her eyes narrowed at me. Her face reddened, and the slight flare of her nostrils was not a good sign.

"I don't understand what's so special about you!" she hollered, her voice louder than I had ever heard from her before.

"What are you even talking about?" I countered, letting go of her arm, needing some space between us—something she didn't want to grant as she took a step forward into my space. Nadine had turned into a little firecracker and I wasn't sure why. I only knew for certain that it was directed at me.

"He's going to pick you," she said, her tone icy, her arms crossed over her chest.

"Who is? Alexander?"

"That is exactly what I'm talking about! You don't even know what is going on and yet you're so special to everyone!" she hollered once more, her hands flying to her side as she stomped her feet.

"To who? I don't know what you are talking about!"

She was frustrated, and I was getting there. So many things didn't make sense, and just when things started to, it all fell to pieces. Who was *everyone*? A heavy sigh escaped me. I barely knew anyone in the castle.

"To Donovan!"

"Donovan…?" I replied, my voice quiet as I stared at her.

The gears in my head spun as I tried to piece together what Donovan had to do with anything. The last time I was with him was when the three of us all went to the bath together. My eyes widened, for his words floated back in my mind. If he wanted me, he would have me. That was what she was talking about?

"He wants you … not me…" Her normal coloring was returning to her face, no longer as red as her hair. But the anger that was once there evaporated and instead left a girl, shoulders quivering as she stared at the ground.

"I don't want him. I told you that."

"It doesn't matter what you want." She turned to walk the last of the distance to the nurse's office. "Donovan gets what he wants … always." Her voice was still quiet but firm.

All I could do was stare at the back of my only friend in the castle. What were we to do? Alexander and I were a perfect match—dare I say a match made in heaven? But it didn't matter within the walls of the castle, for Donovan always got his way and, according to him, Alexander had no power.

"Nadine." My voice shook as I called out to her.

Everything that had happened between Rory and me was being repeated. Instead of me being the one cast aside, left in the cold, it was Nadine. The feelings that must be swarming inside for her were all too real for me.

I followed her. She had already entered the nurse's office, and I paused, my hands on the door, wondering if Amelia had heard. The knowing look she shot in my direction was all the confirmation I needed that she had indeed heard everything that had unfolded in the hallway.

Nadine sat on one of the exam tables, looking out the window. Amelia wheeled herself over to start work on the girl I considered one of my best friends. I sat down at an empty exam table. All I could do was soak in the awkwardness of sitting in silence.

"Morning, ladies." Amelia's voice was hesitant, her hands fast at work, drawing blood from Nadine's arm.

She cast a look my way. I turned away. I'd already tried to talk to Nadine. What she needed was time to cool down, then we could try to settle things between us. Even maybe make a plan so I wouldn't get matched with Donovan.

"You're all set," Amelia said, drawing my attention.

Nadine, with her eyes still cast down, hopped off the exam table and, without a word, left the nurse's office. The door slammed behind her and Amelia wheeled over to my exam table.

"Do you want to explain what's going on?"

"Why wait to ask me when you could have asked Nadine?"

"Because you've already spoken more words than she did today."

I rolled my eyes as I extended my arm, her fingers pressing against my skin before grabbing her supplies to start taking my blood. It was a tiring process, having to get my blood drawn every day. The only upside was they didn't need as much as the first day, so I wasn't too drained. I stared at Amelia's dark eyes. Maybe she could provide some insight on what to do. It wouldn't hurt to at least try.

"Nadine said I was special … and that Donovan was going to pick me."

"Ah, everything makes sense now."

"How does it make sense?" I asked. Even the slight prick on my arm couldn't draw my attention away.

"Nadine likes Donovan."

"Yes, I know that," I replied.

"Yet Donovan wants you."

"That's what I have been told."

"And Donovan gets what Donovan wants," Amelia said as she finished up on my arm, setting things back on her tray.

"Which has been mentioned before, but why?"

"Did you not learn anything from being here?"

My face scrunched, my lips pursing. It was a bit hard to learn what was happening in the castle when so many people omitted things or skirted around answers. Amelia was no different.

"We have one month to find a match, and to find one they have to be compatible with my blood." I waved my hand in the air. This part was common sense. "But Alexander and I are a great match, so it doesn't matter what Donovan wants."

"Because of ranking, Donovan will win." Amelia got up from her seat to make her way to her cabinets in the back of the office.

"But Alexander is practically a prince. How does Donovan outrank him?" I questioned, jumping to my feet.

"I've already said too much."

"How can you scold me for not knowing things, then not tell me things?" I exclaimed, my voice rising at the frustration.

I'd never got the chance to ask Alexander either, too caught up with hands roaming my body.

He wasn't here now and I could focus, but Amelia didn't budge. Her lips pushed tightly together as she walked over to her desk, scribbling away at her papers, not once looking up.

"Fine, be silent about everything," I muttered as I crossed my arms over my chest.

Again, unfazed, Amelia did not look up once. No answers would be shared today.

I entered the hallway in a rush, annoyance and a bit of anger fueling my steps. The hallway provided a quietness that I didn't want, for all I wanted was answers.

"Veronica…"

The hairs on my arm stood up straight, chills running down my back. It was a voice I wasn't familiar with. Moments ago, I'd wished for the quietness to go away, but all I wanted now was for it to come back.

"Veronica," the voice hissed.

"I'm not in the mood to talk," I mumbled as I started walking once more.

Nadine was already upset with me and now a voice was hissing at me in frustration. Fingers wrapped around my arm, and forced to acknowledge whoever lurked in the shadows, I turned, my eyes widening. It was the girl in the light green dress. She was out wandering the halls alone. We were allowed to go to the gathering room and nurse's office without escorts, but that was it. But she wasn't coming from the gathering room. She'd been behind me.

"What are you doing?" I asked.

"You're in danger."

"I've seen you in the nurse's office before."

"Yes, we all go to get our blood drawn."

"That's not what I meant exactly. Why are you here?"

I'd brought up the nurse's office as more of a note that I had seen her before. I may have never talked to her, but I'd seen her within the castle walls.

"You need to listen. You're in danger."

I stared at her. "Yes, you said that. Why am I in danger and from who?"

Her eyes looked crazed, almost glossed over. As I stared at her, I realized she'd been missing from the gathering room lately. Or had I been too preoccupied with Alexander to really notice what was happening around me?

"You can't let him pick you."

"Let who pick me?" I asked, wincing as her fingers dug into my arm.

"Donovan."

"Why, because you want him too?" I bit back, a chuckle escaping.

Karma really had it out for me. I wanted nothing to do with the man, but everyone else was obsessed with him. I jerked my arm out of her hold, rolling my eyes as I started my way back to the gathering room.

But the interaction with the girl in the light green dress reminded me of the girl in the dark green dress. She had looked exactly like the girl behind me. Without thinking, I whirled and looked at the crazed girl.

"Do you have a sister?" I questioned.

"Had."

I frowned as I looked at the girl. Something had happened to make her sister here one day and now no longer part of the living. No announcement of a girl dying had been shared, not one lick of information spilled.

"I must go. Don't let him pick you," she exclaimed as she turned to walk down the dark hallway in the opposite direction of the gathering room.

Marks were visible on her back but quickly fading as she disappeared into the darkness. Before she fully dissolved into the dark, her voice carried on the breeze, dread forming in my heart at her warning.

"Don't let him pick you or you'll end up like my sister."

I knew Donovan was dangerous, but never just how dangerous he could be. If the girl in the light green dress was telling the truth, this had just become a matter of life and death.

Where death was winning, for Donovan always got what he wanted…

Chapter 22

I wanted butterflies in my stomach as I looked upon bright blue eyes, my fingers running through Alexander's smooth blond hair. Instead, I found myself staring into green eyes. Instead of butterflies, it was poison he provided. Looking into his green eyes filled me so much dread, I could hurl. They looked eerily similar to the green dresses the girls wore.

Don't let him pick you or you will end up like my sister.

Dead.

"You don't look happy to see me today."

When did I ever look happy to see him? If he somehow morphed into Alexander, then it would be a different story. But Donovan was Donovan, and he was trouble. I bit down on my tongue, preventing myself from spilling my not-so-nice thoughts. He was the least likely to help my situation, when he was the whole cause of it.

"I figured we could go to my favorite spot today," he said as his lips curled into a smile.

His hand reached out to mine, and before I could move away he'd already grasped my arm, tugging me from my seat and out of the gathering room. Out of the room filled with other people to go onto a ledge several floors above ground.

"Where's Nadine?" I blurted. But more importantly, where was Alexander?

If he'd come for me, then I wouldn't be walking to my doom. Dread bubbled inside to the point it was going to spill over.

"Preoccupied. I wanted to spend some alone time with you."

Too bad no one had asked if I wanted alone time with him. His hold on my arm tightened, his fingers digging into my skin.

"I think Nadine would really like hanging out with us as well." My voice was barely above a whisper. Part of me hoped he didn't hear me, but another part did so he could listen.

"Doesn't matter what she wants."

Because Donovan always gets his way, I repeated in my head. Words that everyone had started to say. Forced to stare at his back as we made our way up the stairs, part of me wondered if I should force the issue more or give up. Everyone else was already on board with my fate being decided, but when there was a blond-haired, blue-eyed man involved, it was hard to give up. With each step we took up the stairs, alarms blared to life in my head. It was a sense of flight or fight, but I could go nowhere due to his grip, his nails digging into my wrist.

We finally made it to the floor to go to the ledge, the feeling of dread back once more. The girl in the light green dress and her sister flashed in my head. She'd said her sister was dead, and I would finally be walking past that room once more. Previously it held three girls, two on either side of the dark green dress girl. As we quickly passed by, there was only one pair of eyes staring at me from a face devoid of emotion. She was alone.

"I didn't plan anything special today, but I figured spending time with me is special enough."

A groan accompanied my rolling eyes. He thought too highly of himself. A special day would be one without him, not one with him. As we walked out on the ledge, he was right. There really was nothing special planned today; the only thing on the ledge was a blanket.

"I heard you like to ask Alex questions. So go ahead, ask me anything."

He made his way over to sit on the blanket, patting the empty space. My eyes narrowed at his words. *Anything* was a loaded word. Just because he said *anything* didn't mean he would be okay with any question.

"Anything?"

"Anything your heart desires," he answered with a smile.

My muscles tensed as I made my way over to sit on the blanket, a spot as far as possible from him without having it look too alarming.

"Why only one match?"

He lay out on his back, folding his arms under his head as he stared into the sky. But no words were uttered as he ignored my question.

There goes the ask anything your heart desires right out the window. I let loose a heavy sigh, tucking my knees into my chest, wrapping my arms around them.

"There aren't enough offerings for all the vampires here. So one match a person."

"So everyone has a chance to pick one match?" I questioned, perking up as he finally provided some information.

"Yes."

"And our opinion doesn't matter?" I pressed.

It was risky going in this direction, but I wanted to be paired with Alexander and not Donovan. He shot a look in my direction, my breathing increasing, for I knew where his thoughts were going.

"It's not like you don't get anything out of being matched. Look around. You get to live in a castle."

A grand castle wasn't everything, especially one that was consumed with darkness and vampires. Those were more the nightmares of children than our dreams. In our dreams, we'd be princesses with free rein to roam the castle and live happily ever after with our princes, ones with bright blue eyes and blond hair. But here? You might find a prince, but there would be no chance of getting him, and the chances of happily-ever-after decreased every day.

"But we don't get a choice?"

"Correct. No choice for you." A smirk was on his face as he sat back up, his green eyes staring straight at me, through me.

"What happens … if we want to be matched with someone else?" I asked, my voice hesitant despite wanting to be firm. It was hard under the man's unwavering stare.

"It doesn't matter."

I couldn't take looking at him anymore. I shifted my attention to the trees outside the castle, the way they swayed in the wind, free outside the castle walls without a care in the world. If only we could switch places. While Donovan was answering my questions, they technically weren't the answers I was looking for. Another sigh escaped. I was delusional to think I would get the answers I wanted.

"You want to be matched with Alexander, don't you?" His voice low and close to my ear. My body stiffened, unable to move, for I hadn't noticed him inch his way into my space. "I thought I told you that if I want you, I will have you. There is nothing your dear Alexander can do about it." His voice was hot on my skin, his touch just as hot as he swiped my hair away from my neck.

I wanted to move, but my body was no longer my own. Fear of the man behind me had taken control, I was trapped in my body, a third party watching my own demise.

His voice was barely a whisper. "I will have you…"

Pain erupted inside me, a searing hot sensation coursing through every part of my body. It spread like wildfire, consuming every part of me. Breathing was hard, the gasps far too spread out. If I didn't get things under control, the dizziness that was creeping in would take control. Then there would be nothing preventing me from tumbling straight over the ledge into the ground below. Nothing but Donovan...

His fingers pressed on my skin, bringing my attention to my neck. That was where the pain was coming from. His hot breath exhaling from his nose had me turning to see. But I wished I hadn't. My breath escaped me once more as Donovan cracked an eye open in my direction. His mouth was tightly pressed to the skin of my neck.

"Get ... off..." I hissed, the burn of bile in the back of my throat teasing to break free.

His fingers, which were just slightly pressed against my skin, turned into a tight hold. His mouth latched on to one side of my neck, held in place by his fingers digging in. The edges of my vision faded to black, and if he didn't let up soon...

His mouth clamped down hard, getting a hiss out of me in response. With Alexander, his bite was passion, igniting something within I didn't even know existed. But Donovan was the exact opposite. If Alexander was the light, Donovan was the darkness, a true monster whose bite could kill you in a flurry of pain.

The thought of the smiling face of Alexander, his blue eyes twinkling at me, filled my mind. I wished it was his hands on my body, his lips pressed against my skin. My eyes shot open. It felt like I was falling, but I didn't want to give up. *I want my happily-ever-after.*

My body protested as I tried to move, jerking, trying to detach the monster's lips.

"I get what I want..." he whispered, his mouth finally off my skin but still close enough to whisper into my ear.

Unable to handle the adrenaline now fading from my system, my body slumped. The arms of the monster wrapped around me, laying me down on the ledge on my back, forcing me to stare up into his face, his green eyes twinkling, smirking proudly. His tongue dipped out and licked at his lips, at my blood. The nausea was back.

He leaned down and placed a lingering kiss on my forehead before entering the castle. The air brushed against my skin. I didn't have the strength to pull myself back to the safety of the castle and off the ledge. A snort escaped, for even thinking the castle was safe. It would never be safe as long as Donovan pined after me. The wind sang a lullaby, allowing my mind to drift away as my vision finally faded. I would rest for a little and hope I didn't fall to my death. Which sounded not too bad at this moment…

CHAPTER 23

My head pounded as I tried to bury myself deeper in the blankets on my bed. The wind grew cold, biting against me, shocking me awake. My energy was still faint but enough had returned to allow me to make it back to my room. My body still burned, the phantom touch of Donovan's fingers and lips still fresh on my neck, sending my mind into panic as I tried to wipe the memory of him, wanting to never relive what had happened on the ledge ever again.

I was late. I should had been at the nurse's office long ago, but the events of last night left little motivation to walk the castle, for if Donovan was someone who had no problem walking the halls in sight, what truly lurked in the darkness of the castle? A shiver ran up my spine. I did my best to smother the dark thoughts, bury them in the back of my mind, but the green eyes of Donovan had awakened me to the darkness all around.

One match. That was all we got, and we didn't even get to have a say. The very worst one had his sights on me. If Donovan wanted me, he would have me. Bile roused in the back of my throat. Could I survive a lifetime at his side? One night alone with him had me at death's door. How many times could I knock before it was finally answered?

Don't let him pick you. The words from the girl in the light green dress floated back through my mind as I threw my legs to the side of the bed, a bitter laugh escaping. It wasn't like I had a choice in the matter. We were prisoners within the walls of this castle.

I ran my fingers through my hair as I calmed my rapidly beating heart. I'd never been this late to the nurse's office before, and I didn't want someone to come looking for me. Namely someone with green eyes. I dragged myself out of bed, out of my room, and straight to the nurse's office. The walk was fast. My mind was in a different place, totally lost as my body moved on autopilot, knocking against the door of the nurse's office, leaning on it as I waited for the okay to enter.

"Come in!" Amelia's voice chimed through the door.

With no time wasted, I made my way over to the exam table. Exhausted from the short walk, vision slightly blurry from pushing myself a bit too much.

"You're later than usual," she said.

Her head was still down as she scribbled on some papers on her desk. My lack of response had her lifting her head up, her eyes widening as she shot to her feet.

"What happened to you?"

My hands flew to my ears, her loud screech sending a wave of pain pulsating through my head.

"Veronica, what happened?" Amelia asked as she made her way over to my bedside.

Her face loomed over mine, her eyebrows drawn together, eyes blinking. I must have looked pretty bad for her to look so concerned.

"Donovan," I bit out, the hate clearly evident in my words.

Her fingers lightly pressed against my chin as she turned my head to expose my neck. She sucked in her breath as she traced the bite, then the other side, where his fingers had dug into my skin.

"It's bruised."

"Is it really bad?"

"Don't worry, I'll take care of you."

"Why did it hurt so bad?" I asked.

Alexander's bite setting my body on fire with passion was the exact opposite of Donovan's bite, setting my body on fire in a way that only brought pain.

"Donovan is … different. He takes pleasure in the pain."

"Just make the pain go away," I groaned out.

One didn't have to be smart to know that Donovan leaned towards the pain side for getting his pleasure.

"Here, drink this." Amelia's voice was soft, and I wasn't sure if it was because I was fading or she was actually speaking softly.

Her arm wrapped around me, supporting me as she brought a cup to my lips. The horrible onslaught on my nose had me jerking my head back, but she held firm, holding me in place.

"What's that smell?" The bile in my throat threatened to come out as she pushed the cup against my lips once more.

"It's a special tonic. Trust me, it will help."

All I could do was shoot her a glare as she tipped the cup to spill the liquid into my mouth. Just like the smell, the taste was absolutely horrible. The liquid trickled down my throat and with every sip I wanted to throw up. But I continued because the warm, disgusting liquid started to soothe my aching body. The tonic she'd created worked its magic, regulating my body once more.

"It's going to make you sleepy, but don't worry. That's just how the tonic works."

"Should've told me this before. I just woke up and now I'm having to go back to sleep," I mumbled out.

My eyelids grew heavy as she moved the cup away from my mouth and helped me back to a lying down position. I could already feel sleep creeping in, just waiting to claim me.

"Veronica!"

My eyes shot open at my name as I looked at the door of the office, where a girl with red hair was getting close. Nadine had come to visit me.

"I heard you were sick."

"From who?" I questioned. The only person I'd had any interaction with so far today was already by my side.

"From Donovan," she answered, causing me to frown.

That was something I wasn't expecting. He'd put me in this state and sent Nadine to check on me?

"And what else did he mention?" I pressed. There had to be a reason she was here.

"What do you mean? He said you got some bug and that I should check in on you."

"So you only checked in on me because he told you to?" I replied, the sick feeling growing inside as I stared at Nadine.

It was a twisted game Donovan was playing, and unfortunately Nadine and I were caught up in it.

"I'm not in the mood to deal with you or Donovan right now," I bit out, resentment growing.

"Deal with me? I came here to check in on you!" Nadine's voice rose, but I didn't care. She wasn't the one in the bed sick.

"Because Donovan told you to! Did he even mention it's because of him that I'm in here like this?"

"You spent time with Donovan?" Her voice, once frustrated, was now hesitant.

I couldn't help the laugh that escaped. It pained my body slightly, but of course that was the only thing important to Nadine. She was worried that I would steal Donovan away from her, despite me telling her I wanted nothing to do with him. I wanted nothing to do with the green-eyed, dark-haired guy, but everything to do with the blond hair and blue eyes of Alexander.

I could hear Nadine talking, but the tonic was kicking into overdrive, carrying me off to dreamland, where I could spend my time with the man I wanted to actually spend my future with and not the monster who threatened to take everything away.

Chapter 24

"Are you feeling better?"

Someone spoke, penetrating the barrier to my dreams, pulling me out and back into reality. A groan escaped me as I opened my eyes, only to shut them tightly from the light beaming down on me.

"How long have I been asleep?" I asked, finally getting my eyes to adjust to the light.

"For several hours. The day's pretty much over," Amelia responded.

It seemed I was still in the nurse's office. My hands clasped the edges of the exam table as I pulled myself to a sitting position. My body was no longer on fire, but it ached slightly. The tonic had worked its magic.

"Alexander stopped by, but you were still asleep so he left."

Alexander had come looking for me? I wondered what he thought when he saw me on the bed, bruised because of Donovan. I pushed off the exam table and planted my feet on the floor. I was a little shaky but needed to get the blood pumping so I could go find him.

"Seems like you're doing a lot better now."

"Thanks to whatever that disgusting tonic was," I replied, as I made my way to leave the nurse's office.

I didn't have time to waste. I had only been away from Alexander for two days, but when one was dropped on death's door and barely crawled back to life, it felt like eternity. My feet pounded against the stone as I made my way to the stairs that would lead me to his bedroom.

We weren't supposed to be out and about in the castle alone, but I didn't care. There was someone I wanted to spend the rest of my life with, and we had things to discuss—namely, how to get me away from Donovan. I could not and would not go through another feeding session with that green-eyed monster. The memory of the way his lips had pressed against my skin, his fingers breaking through the delicate barrier, sent shivers coursing through my body.

I hurled myself towards Alexander's door, slamming my fists on the wood. I could only hope he would be in his room and not out doing something. If so, I would be in trouble. It would be impossible to track him down in the castle. Someone would surely find me first. But my wish was granted when the door flew open. The tousled blond hair with the wide blue eyes staring at me sent warmth flooding through my system. Without a second thought, I embraced the man that filled me with laughter and happiness whenever we were together.

"You're awake…" His voice was husky.

He must have been stirred awake from my abrupt banging. I leaned in, nuzzling my face into his chest as his arms wrapped around my body, swaying us slightly .

"You smell nice." My voice came out muffled. The jitters were slowly going away, eased by his presence.

"I'm glad you are feeling better," he said, his hand coming up to run his fingers through my hair.

I leaned my head back, peering into the light blue eyes that shone down at me. Being with Alexander was all I ever wanted for the rest of life. I loved him…

I broke the contact between us, standing on my toes as I laid a kiss on his lips. A bold move in the middle of the night, but I threw all caution to the wind, for there was nothing to worry about when wrapped in his embrace. His lips pressed against mine before diving in hungrily.

This was what it was supposed to feel like when being matched, passion for one another, not pain. I gasped for air, breaking our kiss as I tilted my head to the side. He got the message. As he carefully pierced the skin of my neck, my body erupted into flames, not caused by pain but by a mix of passion and desire. The bite allowed Alexander to consume me on an intimate level, something I didn't even know was possible before my arrival at the castle.

He had opened my eyes to the wonders that existed in the world, and I wanted to explore it with him at my side. My knees grew weak as I leaned on him heavily. He placed a sweet kiss on the top of my head as he swooped me up, carrying me to the bed so I wouldn't have to walk, which allowed me to stare up at his beautiful face, taking in the moment we shared.

"Thank you," I whispered as he placed me on the bed.

"No, thank *you*," he uttered as he brought me into his chest. "You're absolutely beautiful."

Silence was golden. His mere presence was calming as we lay on the bed. This could be our future, but first I had to get out from Donovan's grasp. I turned on the bed to face Alexander, my hands cupping his face as I stared into his eyes.

"Alexander, are we to be matched?" I asked, my voice wavering slightly.

"I would want nothing else," he answered, leaning in to place a quick kiss upon my lips.

"But is it guaranteed? Can you promise me that? That in the end it will be you and me?" I pressed on, pushing my body against his.

"I promise I will do my best to see that we are matched."

He would do his best, but that wasn't a guarantee. As Alexander's eyes drifted closed, a pair of green eyes that belonged to Donovan formed behind him. I knew it was my mind playing tricks on me, but it was so lifelike, the smirk on his face sending shivers down my spine. I tore away from the image, it disappearing as I stared at Alexander. He could be my future, but Donovan got what he wanted, and he wanted me. There was nothing Alexander could do about it.

CHAPTER 25

The tension in the air was palpable as I sat next to Nadine in the gathering room. By the glances they shot in our direction, I could tell the other girls could read the strained friendship between us. No one dared to utter a word, but what could they say? They steered clear of Nadine because of the questionable company she kept, which limited my chances to form other bonds out of a sense of loyalty to the first girl to talk to me.

Now we were both stuck without someone to talk to. My gaze drifted over to the girl in the pale green dress, who stood in a corner. I wanted to ask her more questions, but that would be impossible; the topic of Donovan was a sensitive one with Nadine around. I would be forced to wait for her to leave, but the only person who came to get her was Donovan. A string of curses flew under my breath, for if Donovan came to get her, then surely he would take me along as well.

Nadine got up from her seat on the pillows. The feeling in my chest was heavy as I got up from my seat as well, but unlike Nadine I didn't make my way towards the door to leave, but attempted to slink off into the corner. Another slew of curses escaped under my breath as, barely caught from the corner of my eye, was the girl in the light green dress, standing still with wide eyes. I didn't know everyone she was afraid of, but there was one I knew of that could spark fear in her.

"Veronica..." Donovan's deep voice paused my attempt to hide, my body betraying me and mimicking the girl.

A tight pressure, accompanied by nails digging into my skin, had me wincing, attempting to jerk my arm out of its cage. I pulled my arm once more, but his hold didn't budge. Instead he jerked it, turning me.

"I see you're feeling well." His eyes narrowed as his lips thinly pressed together.

A sneer with a slight hiss escaped from Donovan; his hold tightened even more. At this rate, he would cut off circulation to my wrist.

"I have plans for the three of us today." He made his way to the door, me in tow.

"I'm coming as well?" Nadine asked as we passed her.

She wasted no time in latching herself on to the other side of the man. I could only stare at her as she looked at him as if she was seeing the most amazing man in the world. Was she so in love that she couldn't even see me in pain right next to her? Her presence caused him to shift his hold on my wrist as he wrapped his free arm around Nadine's waist. He brought her in close, placing a hungry kiss on her lips, all for those in the gathering room to see as well.

"Actually," a new but very familiar voice chimed in, "Veronica has a few more tests she needs to get done. So she'll be coming with me."

I jerked my head in the direction of the voice, a smile forming, for Amelia had come to save me. Her slender frame slid through the door, a clipboard in hand.

The silence in the room was deafening. Donovan stared at Amelia. His hold loosened till finally his arm dropped away. I cradled my throbbing wrist to my chest as I followed the nurse out into the hallway.

"I didn't know I needed additional tests," I whispered, doing my best to keep my voice as low as possible but loud enough for her to still hear me.

"You don't," she said as she shot a smile over her shoulder. "Don't expect another save from me though. Now, don't speak till we get to the office," she continued on, not breaking her stride as we made our way down the hallway to her office.

She didn't have to tell me twice to not speak. Donovan and Nadine would have left the gathering room shortly after us, and it would just be my bad luck to have them venture down the same path.

"You didn't fight me on this, which is surprising." Amelia made her way to sit at her desk now that we'd entered her office.

"The only other option I had was to spend the day with Donovan. I'm not too eager to have a repeat of what happened last time…" I grumbled.

"If Donovan got his fill from you today, I'm afraid you probably wouldn't be waking up tomorrow."

I shrugged off her comment as I sat down at the exam table. There wasn't much one could do when being told that they could have died today. Everything in this castle was darkness trying to swallow me whole—except for one man who ignited a fire within me.

"Is Alexander busy today?" I asked.

Amelia didn't look up from her desk as she continued working on whatever kept her occupied the majority of the time I entered her office.

After a long pause, she finally spoke, but all it did was fill my stomach with dread. "Donovan paid him a visit."

My palms grew sweaty as I gripped the edges of the exam table. All I could do was stare. Donovan would have won if a fight broke out, which meant Alexander might be hurt.

"Relax, no one is injured."

"What happened when Donovan visited Alexander?" I asked, my words coming out fast.

"Donovan was staking his claim."

There was a lump in my throat. I tried to swallow it down so I could speak, but I was rendered speechless. There was no need to ask what he was staking his claim on.

"Donovan gets what he wants…" I whispered.

Amelia finally looked up from her papers to look at me, her lips pressed together in a slight grimace.

A tightness formed in my chest. "It has been etched in my brain that Donovan gets what he wants. But why when Alexander is basically a prince?"

"In name yes, Alexander is a prince. But he's a prince without power. He refused the trials and now he's a puppet."

"Trials?" I questioned.

"There is a lot about us you have yet to learn. Things we aren't willing to share. Things not shared in that book Alexander gave you."

I stared at Amelia. She knew a lot of things. Like how Alexander had given me a vampire book to read on our first date. I was sure we were alone in a field of flowers.

"You seem to be aware of a lot of things that happen in this castle," I bit out, my eyes narrowing..

"Don't worry. I'm not an enemy." Her lips curled into a smile as she waved her hands in the air to help decrease the tension forming.

That wasn't exactly the response I was looking for, but I did settle down slightly. If she was truly the enemy, she wouldn't have come for me and provided an escape from Donovan's clutches.

"There's no way for Alexander to claim me over Donovan?"

She answered with a simple no, not instilling much confidence that I could change my future.

"So I will be matched with Donovan, and I have no way out?"

"It seems so. Too bad your other match never came forward," she muttered as she once more wrote away on her papers on her desk.

But her words caused the gears twisting in my mind to slam to a halt. She'd previously told me I had more than one match, but never actually stated how many matches I had. But she had slipped; there was a third match out there. Based on the way she said it, it sounded like he could outrank Donovan. I pushed off the exam table, landing on the floor with a thud as I sprinted the short distance toward her. My hands slammed on the desk, rattling her papers slightly, as she looked up at me, her eyes wide.

"A third match? Who is it?"

"Sebastian…"

"Who is Sebastian?" I hadn't met a Sebastian in the castle…

Amelia leaned back in her chair as she crossed her arms over her chest. She sized me up, but I didn't back down. This was information I needed to know if I wanted any chance of escaping from Donovan's clutches. She let loose a heavy sigh as she leaned in. My body tensed as I waited for her to talk.

"The one who was sent to retrieve you."

The image of a man with slick, straight, silver hair leaning against a tree, his silver eyes staring at me as I swam, flashed through my mind. That was Sebastian? His name rolled off my tongue quietly, smoothly. Judging by our short time together, he seemed one hundred percent better than Donovan.

"But he won't claim you. He never claims anyone," Amelia muttered, attempting to shatter my chance at freedom.

That he never claimed anyone was about to be put to the test, because I was desperate. My life was on the line and he was my only chance at saving it.

With new resolve, I stared into Amelia's eyes. "How do I find Sebastian?"

Chapter 26

I brought my arm up to cover my eyes as I fell back onto my bed. The rest of the day had to be spent helping Amelia or it would look suspicious. If I didn't stay around and help, then I would have to go back to the gathering room, where I would potentially have to spend time with Donovan.

I rubbed my eyes. Amelia had shared some information about Sebastian. The biggest piece was that he wasn't in the castle today. So any plans of tracking him down were thrown out the window.

Time was not on my side. I couldn't wait around for several days waiting for his return. I grabbed hold of my blanket, wrapping myself up in its warmth as I tried to relax. I did have a *bit* of time. The one month wasn't up. All I had to do was keep avoiding Donovan.

A snort escaped. That was easier said than done. The lids of my eyes grew heavy, the exhaustion from the day finally settling in. Just because Amelia had saved me didn't mean I was sitting around all day. No, she had put me to work. She had to sell it after all, for both our sakes.

I groaned, wishing there was someone next to me, someone with blond hair and beautiful bright blue eyes who goes by the name of Alexander. When the days were filled with darkness, all I wanted was a taste of the light. For that, I would have to track down Alexander, but I was too tired at the moment. Tomorrow, though, would be a new day, and I would go see him. After a long night of rest. My body agreed and my eyes grew too heavy to keep open.

My eyes shot open, my heart rate increasing at the sound of a creak. The rapid beating of my heart thumped so loudly in my ears I almost missed the noise, leaving my body momently paralyzed at not only the fear but the shock of the unknown.

"I know you're awake."

All sense of time slowed, but I knew it was the fear. My mind urged me to run, but my body was still coming to, momentarily disabled from the shock of hearing Donovan's voice.

"Are you going to pretend you're asleep?" His deep voice was closer than before.

I jerked up, scooting myself away from him, my body finally responding to my urges to move. It was naïve to think Amelia had saved me for the day.

Donovan gets what Donovan wants.

My bed let out a groan from the added weight as he invited himself to sit on the edge. His hand reached out to caress my leg under the sheets. I never thought Donovan would seek me out and come to my room. And for my mistake I was about to pay an unfortunate price. I should have known better. He was a monster after all.

"Are you done playing games?" His voice was low, slicing through the air.

His patience was wearing thin, and I was the source of his anger. With no other in the room to divide his attention, I would be forced to bear the brute force of what was to follow. I quickly glanced at the door before looking at Donovan. It wasn't smart to take one's eyes off the enemy, but I needed to see if there was a way to escape. Internally I swore, for if I was to lunge for the door, I would have to pass right over him. He wouldn't even need to get up to trap me. I would be making it too easy for him.

"Don't get any crazy ideas," he taunted.

"Why are you here?" I blurted, my voice cracking.

A smile formed on his face. He knew the effect he was having on me. "Why do you think I am here?" he said, inching closer to me.

Did he really think I was going to answer that? Why speak something into existence when I didn't want it to happen? His lips parted, drawing in a long breath. His body fidgeted as he reached out to me.

"I think you should leave."

I didn't sound convincing, couldn't even soothe my own mind into believing the words uttered from my lips. His eyes narrowed in response, his lips curving into a sneer. My heart beat so fast it was going to burst through my chest if this moment lingered on too long. Everything shifted to an even worse nightmare as his hand reached out, clasping my throat, squeezing.

I gripped on to him, trying to pry him off. My breath came out in gasps as my head got light, but the green eyes of the monster before me never faded. Donovan and I were in my room alone. There would be no one coming to rescue me. No one knew he was here.

My gaze drifted to the door, still cracked from his entry. If only I could make my way over there. Then, just maybe, I could find someone to help. His hand still clutched tightly around my neck as the other gripped my leg, pulling me down and away from my corner. His green eyes gazed into me as he leaned over me. I had no control of my actions, my energy rapidly fading as I tried to focus on breathing, impossible to do with his hand still clutched tightly. I didn't want to look at him. I didn't want to see the green eyes, opting to stare into the darkness of the hallway that lay outside of the cracked door. The darkness sounded a lot more comforting and appealing than before.

A flash of silver hair followed by silver eyes staring straight into me sent a jolt through my body. The pressure on my neck and lack of oxygen was too much. I was starting to hallucinate. Donovan shifted, leaning his face into the crook of my neck, his hot breath against my skin raising goosebumps.

Amelia had said if Donovan got another feeding session from me, I wouldn't survive. My mind screamed to push him away, but my body didn't respond. It wasn't my own. I had lost control over it a long time ago. A prisoner trapped in my own body, held hostage by a monster with piercing green eyes that would forever haunt me, in life or death. Accepting my fate, I allowed the hold around me to finally submerge me into the darkness.

There would be no one coming to save me.

CHAPTER 27

My head throbbed with uncontrollable pain as I rolled over in bed. It seemed most days were now spent in some type of pain, all thanks to Donovan. Events from last night were still vivid in my mind. I would never forget his green eyes. They were starting to become the fuel for my nightmares. Thankfully, I had passed out before his teeth pierced my skin, so I wouldn't have to remember that piece, but a shiver coursed through my body as I brought the blankets further up my body, doing my best to wrap myself up. The silky navy-blue sheets rubbed against me as I shifted once more.

I gazed down. I didn't have navy-blue silk sheets.

I shot up out of bed as I brought the sheets up to my face to examine them closer. My room only came with black sheets, yet today it was a mix of black and blue. Panic surged inside at the realization someone else had been in my room other than Donovan.

"Seems you're awake…" The voice that spoke was soft, only vaguely familiar—I couldn't place it. The only thing was that it didn't belong to either Alexander of Donovan. I turned to where the voice was coming from, my eyes widening.

"Sebastian," I whispered.

The man who could make all my problems disappear.

"It seems like Amelia has been talking more than she should."

"Only because no one else has been telling me things," I bit back, moving myself to the edge of my bed.

"Why do you feel entitled to know things?" he replied, crossing his arms over his chest. "If I'm not mistaken, I told you where to find your sister that one night."

"Yes, which started a chain reaction, and that's how I found myself here," I bit out, waving my hands in the air.

Sebastian leaned back in the chair he occupied, propping his feet up on the edges of my bed as he stared at me.

"Making yourself at home?"

"I do live here after all."

I scowled at him, unamused by his response or his nonchalant attitude. Since the conversation wasn't going anywhere productive, I took the moment to examine him. He wore different clothes than when I had first met him back in my village. His hair framed his face while the rest was pulled into a low ponytail at the back of his head. Tight black pants coupled with a sleeveless tight black shirt had him almost blending with the darkness, but his silver features were a dead giveaway. His frame was a mix between Donovan, where he wasn't too big, and Alexander, where he wasn't too thin.

"What happened last night?" I kept my voice low as I stared into his silver eyes.

"Nothing."

"What do you mean, nothing? Donovan was here!"

"Nothing happened. He left after you passed out."

"Because of you?" I asked.

I'd thought it was a hallucination when I'd gleaned the silver in the darkness, but he had truly been there last night.

He didn't reply, only shifting his gaze away from my direction, and I knew it was because of him that Donovan had left.

"I have things I got to do." He got up from his seat, reaching down to grab something by the chair, throwing it on the bed in front of me.

Realization dawned immediately, for it was my bag that I'd left home with. I didn't get to keep my bag on arrival because he had taken it with him when he'd walked off into the darkness.

"I need a favor from you," I exclaimed, grabbing hold of the bag and dragging it closer to my body.

Sebastian didn't leave, but paused to look over his shoulder.

My cue to ask for my favor: "I need you to pick me as your match."

"I can not," he replied curtly.

"Why not?" My voice rose in pitch as I stared at his back.

The man before me was my only hope. Ideally, I would have wanted Alexander to pick me, but he couldn't outrank Donovan. But the silver-haired man with equally silver eyes did outrank the monster.

"I can't protect you."

"What do you mean? Why is everyone so cryptic here? Just say what it!" I yelled, my face heating up.

He turned to me, a frown on his face. "I'm a retriever. We leave the castle to retrieve those that are offered. I would rarely be in the castle to protect you from the others."

"That's fine. That actually works out. I will just stay with Alexander."

"And that is exactly why," he replied, pushing the hair that framed his face out of the way.

With a heavy sigh, he headed towards my door. But I wasn't done with the conversation. I wasn't sure when I would see Sebastian next, and I needed to get him on board now rather than later.

"Why is that an issue?" I blurted out.

"Because I don't share," he replied as he walked out of my room, not even sending a look over his shoulder in my direction.

I stared at the empty space. I had no way of finding him again. No information about where in the castle he slept or where he hung out. But at least he'd brought me my bag. I opened the sack, sticking my hand in, my fingers grabbing hold of something familiar. I'd barely used it—I never had the time, since it was a wedding gift, but now it would be put to good use. A smile formed on my face as I yanked the dagger from my bag.

If no one was going to save me, I was going to save myself.

Chapter 28

For, the first time in a while, sleep came easy. It might have been due to the jitters from what would happen today, or because I had the safety of my dagger now. I would no longer have uninvited guests at night. My sheets tumbled to the ground as I jumped out of bed. I had to get my day started. My hands pulled at my sheets, ripping off a piece. One small enough to tie my dagger to the side but slightly on my back. Unfortunately, as the dresses they made us wear left very little to the imagination, that meant barely any places to hide a dagger. My feet went on autopilot, leading me out of my room and straight to the nurse's office.

By some twist of fate, I'd ended up with three matches. A man with blond hair and blue eyes, the one forbidden to me. Another with equally silver hair and eyes, the one who did not want me. And finally, the monster obsessed with me.

Neither of the first two men were to be my knight in shining armor to whisk me away from this nightmare. But with my dagger at my side, I was no longer defenseless. I would be ready to battle whatever came my way.

"Come in," Amelia called out after my fist rapped against the door. Upon entering the office, I headed straight to the exam table, doing my best to make sure my walking wasn't weird, that it didn't look like I had a dagger attached to my side. Carefully adjusting my body so I could sit on the exam table, I waited for the daily dose of blood withdrawal. Amelia looked up from her papers, a smile on her face as she wheeled herself over to my side.

"I heard you got in contact with Sebastian."

"I did." My answer was shorter than I'd intended, but her tug on my arm caused a light jerk in my body.

My movements needed to be careful in order for the dagger to not be seen, and having her tugging on my arm certainty didn't help. I couldn't lose my dagger. Without it, I would be in the same position as the last few days, unable to fend off Donovan.

"You aren't asking your usual questions," she muttered, her hands pausing in their work.

"There's nothing to talk about," I replied.

Her eyebrows shot up, her eyes widening as she stared at me. I kept my face neutral to not betray my thoughts.

"Something is off." She paused as she scooted back on her stool. "Whatever you're thinking, it's a bad idea." She crossed her arms over her chest as she stared into my eyes.

"I don't know what you're talking about."

"You haven't asked about Alexander. You haven't mentioned any details about your meeting with Sebastian. More importantly, you haven't talked about your encounter with Donovan!"

"You seem to know everything already. Why do I need to explain it?" I crossed my arms, too, my eyes narrowing as I stared back at her.

"There's a lot to be learned if one asks the right questions and talks to the right people. It also helps that I'm friendly," she replied, getting up from her seat to go behind her desk. "So, Veronica, what's on your mind?"

"I don't think I should be saying in your presence."

If anyone got wind that I held a dagger, they would take it away from me. My only way of protecting myself would be gone. I couldn't let that happen.

"We aren't all like Donovan," Amelia whispered, her lips pursed together.

"Being a bystander is just as bad as being like Donovan."

I pushed off the exam table, doing my best not to expose the dagger held to my side as I made my way to the door. My retort might have been harsh, but it was the truth.

Everyone knew the fate that awaited me if I were to match with Donovan. Everyone knew from the beginning, but no one had opted to share that information until it was too late. It took arriving at death's door and returning for people to start to care. If she had told me about Sebastian earlier, this all could have been avoided. If Sebastian had come for me earlier, returned my bag sooner, then maybe Donovan would have had second thoughts about picking me. But it was too late; the dice were cast and my fate was sealed.

"Don't do it." Amelia's warning caused me to pause with my hand pressed against the door.

"You don't even know what I'm thinking about, let alone what I'm about to do."

"No, I don't. I just know whatever it is, you will regret it."

I entered the hallway to go to the gathering room. She was wrong. I would not regret my actions. What I would regret would be being chained to Donovan, and what would surely follow when one became a pet to a monster.

All my life, I had put others first. I had agreed to marry Jax so Rory could live her dream of exploring the world outside of our town. And when she fell in love with my soon-to-be husband, I switched places with her—why condemn all of us to misery when they could have their happily ever after? Today I would finally be putting myself first. I deserved a happy ending, and to have one, Donovan must go.

"Donovan has requested you today," Nadine chimed as I slid into the gathering room.

"Did he say where?" I replied.

The time had come. It was do or die, and I had no intention of dying.

Chapter 29

Of course, it had to be the ledge. Donovan's favorite place. It was only fitting that he wanted to meet up there again for another date.

Donovan didn't come to fetch me, opting instead to have Nadine tell me where to go. I was thankful for it, because he was too observant, too touchy. He would have surely felt the dagger attached to my side, and then he would have the upper hand. I ascended the stairs slowly, wishing time could just slow. My pounding heart filled the silence.

I could run to Alexander and avoid Donovan, but that would only ignite his ire. Time with Alexander also clouded my judgment, changed my mind. One minute I would be determined to do something and the next he would have his hands on my body, that sweet smile of his with those bright blue eyes setting me aflame with desire. No, going to Alexander would be too much of a distraction.

Finally arriving on the floor that contained the ledge to the outside, I paused at the door, which was cracked open. Before, it had contained the girls, in particular the one with the dark green dress, but today there were no girls in there. I couldn't help but frown as I pushed the door open wider to get a better look inside.

There was no bed, no comforts at all in the room, yet there used to be three girls in there.

"What are you doing?"

I jerked back, the voice scaring me. From the corner of my eye, Donovan emerged from the door that led to the ledge where we'd had our first date.

"Someone is too curious." He leaned against the wall, his arms crossing over his chest, a smile on his face.

"Nadine said you requested me."

"I did. I had half a thought that you wouldn't show up and I would have to hunt you down. Too bad … I was looking forward to the fun." He motioned to the open door.

With my eyes glued to his, I made my way to him and the open door, only pausing briefly to stand before him before going out on the ledge. Just like last time, the wind blew against my skin. It was going to be a cold one today—the perfect mood to match my feelings. His hand pressed against my exposed back only centimeters away from my dagger, my body stiffening in response. If his hand traveled just a bit, I would be caught. Adrenaline shot through my body as I whirled on him, his hand falling to his side as I faced him.

"Do we have anything planned for the date today?" I asked, taking a step back, my hand trailing the castle wall to make sure I didn't fall. He stepped forward, making sure space between us was nonexistent. With each step back I took, he made a step forward.

"Nothing other than having my fill," he smirked, the curl of his lips sending jolts through my body.

I wanted to flee, but there was nowhere to go. Donovan blocked the exit; all that lay behind me was more ledge. His hands cupped my cheeks as he leaned in, placing a kiss on my lips before hungrily diving in, exploring. I didn't engage, but that didn't deter him though. He pushed against my body as if we were lovers. My knees buckled from the force of him on me, him guiding me to lie on the ledge.

My head pounded with the sounds of my heartbeat. Could he hear how panicked I was? He broke away, putting some distance between us but still hovering over me.

"It's not fun if you don't engage. At least put up some kind of fight," he whispered, his deep voice rattling my nerves.

My arm brushed against my side and the feel of the dagger brought peace of mind, suppressing my previous fears. I'd almost forgotten about it.

I stared at the green eyes that stared back at me as I inched my hands up to my side so I could get a better grip on my dagger. A smile spread on Donovan's face, for his prey was moving, engaging finally. But he'd read everything wrong.

His hands gripped his shirt, lifting it above his head, and it was that second when his gaze was blocked that I gripped my dagger, tucking it under my thigh.

"Not so bad now, is it?"

He leaned in once more, nuzzling my neck. The proximity was sending my heart into overdrive again. All I needed to do was focus on the dagger and I could do this. I could break free from the chains before they even got to be placed on me.

His breath hot against my skin, I could feel his lips parting, his tongue swiping out to brush against my skin. He was so into this. My stomach dropped, my limbs feeling heavy as a sour taste settled in my mouth. I needed to close my eyes. It was too much. When his wet tongue disappeared … the moment before he dived into my neck for his meal … that's when I would strike. He would be too focused on enjoying the situation, making him less aware of everything else unfolding around him. At least, that was what I told myself.

"Now, just sit back and enjoy." His voice was low, muffled from how close to my skin he was.

My fingers wrapped around the dagger's grip, my leg arching to allow me easier access. Donovan let out a throaty laugh as my leg pressed into him. Did he think I was enjoying this? A burning in my throat formed at his reaction. Once more, he pressed his lips to my neck.

My eyes shot open.

Body on autopilot, I yanked the dagger out of the scabbard and plunged it straight into his back. Donovan jerked for a moment. Adrenaline coursed through my veins. He made an attempt to dislodge himself from me, but he'd nuzzled himself to the point that it wasn't that easy.

Especially when on a ledge with no barrier to stop one from falling.

"What … did you do?" His voice was fueled with anger, fueling me even more. I removed the dagger from his back only to plunge it in it once more. But I didn't stop. I'd never learned how to kill a vampire. That was knowledge they kept secret, but I would keep going, plunging my dagger over and over, till my arm gave out if I had to. It was life or death. Him or me. And it wasn't going to be me.

His hands gripped my sides as he pushed up, but I clung on to him, not wanting to put distance between us and give him the chance to take control.

"You … you…" he mumbled, his eyes wide, but there was a far-off, distant look to him. He wasn't totally here anymore, and after a few more stabs maybe he would finally leave the world. It was getting harder to keep going. I had to switch from stabbing him in the back to actually doing it in his chest.

Forced now to watch his eyes track my movements, I reeled my arm back, and when I plunged it forward, burying my dagger in his chest, liquid splattered with every stab, but I couldn't focus on it; it would distract me. A single distraction could change the tide. After all, it was when he pulled his shirt off, covering his eyes only briefly, that allowed me to be able to take him on.

His hands shook as he brought them up to his chest, grabbing the handle of the dagger, trying to stop me. But he was too weak. Even with his hands wrapped around mine, I was still in control. Still able to pull it out and plunge it in once more. This time, though, his body jerked, his eyes glazed, and time stopped.

It wasn't a beautiful moment, seeing him trying to cling to life but unable to. But it also wasn't a moment that would haunt my dreams.

I removed the dagger slowly, gripping into his shoulder as I plunged it in once more. This time, there was no resistance. With a slight push, he fell back, landing on the edge. It wasn't enough to keep him up here with me. Donovan's body sank through the air, his body lifeless and unmoving.

Watching him disappear from my life had the adrenaline leaving my body. The worst of it was over. The silence, only broken by sounds from nature, calmed me as I lay out on the ledge. It would be best to make my way back inside, wash up. But I couldn't. While my mind was calming down, being clearer, my body twitched, still trying to come to terms with no longer being in a life-or-death situation.

All I needed was some time, a little rest, then I could figure out what was next. I had a whole life to look forward to.

Chapter 30

My body hurt. A groan escaped as I rolled over. My eyes shot open.

The last place I remembered being was on the ledge, but now I was in the gathering room. Thankfully, I hadn't plunged to my death like Donovan. But who'd found me and brought me inside?

"Glad to see you are awake..." a voice murmured from somewhere in the room. It was dark. The moonlight that shone through the glass helped, but pitch-black darkness was a specialty of this place. Silver hair emerged from the shadows, the man's eyes silver, his face tight, no emotion shown, as he made his way to my side.

"You made a horrible mistake." His voice was still low, his arms crossing over his chest as he stopped in front of me.

It forced me to tilt my head up to look at him, his eyes staring straight into mine.

"You can't just kill a vampire."

"What else did you expect me to do?"

"Anything but kill the man," he growled as he crouched, coming level with me.

"There was no other option! Alexander can't claim me. You won't claim me! I couldn't let Donovan claim me … it was life or death." Passion fueled my words, making them stronger than intended.

"It wouldn't have come to that…"

"Nothing made it seem so. Amelia warning me and the girl in the light green dress… Everyone told me to stay away from him, and I tried."

"You need to shower, we have somewhere to be," Sebastian murmured as he got up once more, leaving me alone on the ground.

"Where are we going?"

"You can't just kill a vampire and expect people not to notice." His hand grabbed on to my elbow, tugging me to stand on my feet.

There was no point in resisting. I needed a shower badly. Dried blood caked my body. I wanted it off. Any memory of Donovan needed to be wiped.

Sebastian walked me into the bathroom, closing the door behind me. It was quiet. No other girls were present. My reflection stared back at me as I walked towards the stall. It looked like me, but it also didn't.

I never thought I would have a moment like this in my life, where I would have to take another's life. I gripped the straps of my dress, sending it to the floor as I stepped into the shower. Water blasted on, burning at my skin. The process of rubbing out the blood was a slow one. I didn't want to leave a single speck behind.

When finally I was content with rubbing a layer of skin off, I turned the shower off. With a quick dry off with a towel, and dressed in the spare dress placed on the counter, I was ready to face what was next. Whatever that was.

"The Grand Elder has called a meeting about your actions," Sebastian said as I emerged from the showers, already heading straight to the doors to leave the gathering room.

"The other girls will be there?" I asked, forced to follow behind him. I'd already upset the balance and didn't need to be on another vampire's bad side.

"No. Your audience will be vampires today. The girls will wake up tomorrow and go to the gathering room as normal, but you won't be there."

"I'll just disappear in the night? What about Nadine? Where am I going?"

"I don't know. It's up to the Grand Elder. What I do know is your life is going to get a lot worse..." Sebastien shot a look over his shoulder as we crossed the last of the distance to the door, to the same place I'd seen the Grand Elder my first night here. Instead of having a line of other girls with me, I would be his sole focus tonight. A lump formed in my throat at the thought of being the center of attention.

The doors creaked open, Sebastien quickly walking in and joining the crowd that was waiting in the darkness. Hairs lifted on the back of my neck as I stepped into the room, all eyes watching every step I took. There were a lot of vampires in the room, a lot more than I had seen in the castle during my short time here. All ranges of people were here, some females, some males. A few were short, but the majority of them tall. Some even looked like the walking dead, almost rivaling the Grand Elder with his pale and dark features. A part of me wanted to investigate them, but another part of me wished I wasn't the center of their attention.

"Veronica."

That voice was hard to forget. The Grand Elder made his way forward, away from the people who stood by his side.

"It was such a surprise to hear about what you'd done. Especially since it was Donovan." A laugh escaped from the Grand Elder as he stopped right in front of me, his beady black eyes staring straight into mine. The chills in my body spreading the longer we held eye contact.

"Such a feisty human … who would've thought," he said as he walked around me. "Don't think we've had one like you in a long time." He stopped once more in front of me. "But tell me, girl, what drove you to do such a thing?" His hand came out to cup my chin as he tilted my head to one side and the other.

I jerked myself back out of his hold, a smirk spreading on his face at my action.

"Kill me too, like you did, Donovan? Not going to work."

I could tell by the way he was talking that he was amused. That my life could have been lost tonight if Donovan had his way had no impact on him. My lips turned into a frown. We were just offerings to the vampires, after all. They didn't care what happen to us. The only vampire who burned with light instead of hiding in the darkness was Alexander. He was the whole reason I'd wanted away from Donovan. For me to have a happy life.

"Well? I asked a question."

"I didn't want to be matched with him." My words caused the man before me to burst into laughter once more.

"All of that just because you didn't want to be matched? No, there was a reason you fought back so hard. So tell me girl, what was it?"

A figure emerged from the darkness where the Grand Elder had once stood, my heartbeat increasing at seeing the blond hair and blue eyes of Alexander. He was here? A fluttering feeling formed in my chest as I shifted back to the Grand Elder. With Alexander by my side, anything could be possible.

"There was another."

"Another you wanted to be matched to?"

"Yes."

"And please tell, who is that? I would certainty like to know who drove you to commit such violence."

But I didn't want to answer. His eyes narrowed as my gaze shifted towards the ground. Fingers dug into the skin of my neck as the Grand Elder wrapped a hand around it, forcing me to look back up at him.

"When I ask a question, you answer."

My heart raced, my hands jumping to pry his hold off me, but somehow I still managed to squeak out the name of my blue-eyed love. I smacked into the floor. The Grand Elder took a few steps back after he dropped his hold on me.

"My son? Oh, that's rich!" he shouted, followed by a laugh as he motioned for Alexander to come forward. I locked on to Alexander, watching his every step. His face was neutral, not betraying anything as he made his way to stand next to his father.

"Alexander, will you match with her?"

I shifted my gaze over to Alexander, who refused to look at me, his eyes on the ground covered by his hair.

"No."

My head pounded, unable to figure out his response, an ache forming in my heart. "No...?" I murmured. My voice was quiet, barely above a whisper. I'd lost that strong tone that I'd used just moments ago. My world was shifting, and it wasn't for the better.

"No ... I was attracted to you because you were human." Alexander finally looked up at me, his eyes cold, eyebrows low as he held my gaze. "But you are just a monster."

Laughter filled the air, breaking through the silence that was forming. I was unable to form any response, his cold dead eyes freezing my body.

"You see, Alexander doesn't like to embrace his vampire heritage, and by you killing Donovan, you are more like us than the humans he admires."

"I ... I don't understand..." I couldn't tear my gaze away from Alexander. My eyes grew wet, vision starting to blur, still trying to understand the twisted turn of events.

"I can't love someone who has killed another," Alexander whispered, kneeling in front of me, his hand reaching out to my neck, wrapping around the necklace he'd given me.

With a tug, it fell away, and with it I felt a part of myself leaving as well.

"You were supposed to me my sun, a light in this dark castle. But you're just darkness as well," he muttered, standing up and turning his back on me.

I wanted to reach out to him, but I was paralyzed. I had done what I did so I could be with him since he couldn't outrank Donovan. By grasping my destiny in my own hands, I had shattered any chance of being with him.

"Well, Veronica … what should we do with you?" the Grand Elder asked next to me, my gaze still focused on the retreating back of the blond-haired man who had filled me with happiness. "With no match, we would usually just kill you."

His hand came out to pet the side of my head. "But you killed a vampire, so we can't just get rid of you." His hand dropped below my chin, cupping it as he tilted my head to look at him. "No, I have the perfect punishment for you." His fingers squeezed my chin while his lips curved into a smile.

"You're going to partake in the blood trials."

The adventure is not over and I hope you forgive me for the cliffhanger!

Continue the adventure by buying book two! Make sure to sign up for my newsletter to get alerted with news and secret prizes!

Website: www.mazeleigh.com

As a new author, reviews are of supreme importance to my success. If you have a moment to leave a review please do so! Every review helps!

About Maze Leigh

Desk job worker by day and writer by night, Maze Leigh is obsessed with all things fantasy. The good, the bad, and everything in between. She is partial to magic as it helps explain the unknowns of the world. Coupled with her overactive imagination, there is no limit to the stories she tells.

Make sure to sign-up for the newsletter to get updates and secret prizes!

You can also stalk Maze on several social media sites and they can be found by going to the links page on her website!

Website: www.mazeleigh.com

www.ingramcontent.com/pod-product-compliance
Lightning Source LLC
Chambersburg PA
CBHW030633190726
48286CB00008B/2513